LOVE BEGINS AT GOLDEN SANDS BAY

THE GOLDEN SANDS BAY SERIES - BOOK TWO

GEORGINA TROY

Boldwood

First published in 2018. This edition first published in Great Britain in 2023 by Boldwood Books Ltd.

Cover Design by Alexandra Allden

Cover Photography: Shutterstock

A CIP catalogue record for this book is available from the British Library.

Paperback ISBN 978-1-80426-057-9

Large Print ISBN 978-1-80426-058-6

Hardback ISBN 978-1-80426-059-3

Ebook ISBN 978-1-80426-056-2

Kindle ISBN 978-1-80426-055-5

Audio CD ISBN 978-1-80426-064-7

MP3 CD ISBN 978-1-80426-063-0

Digital audio download ISBN 978-1-80426-060-9

Boldwood Books Ltd
23 Bowerdean Street
London SW6 3TN
www.boldwoodbooks.com

To my son James, with love.

1

LONDON – OCTOBER

'What the bleedin' 'ell are you doin'?' the rudest celebrity Bella had ever had the misfortune to work with asked, elbowing her in the ribs.

Bella gasped in pain and drew back. 'If you want it to appear as if my hands belong to you then I have to reach around you. You know that.'

She rubbed her side. It had been a long hour waiting for Megan Knight to have her hair and make-up done to her satisfaction and Bella wasn't sure how long she could keep her temper under control. She had been a hand model for fifty plus celebrities over the past eight years. The part-time work had been reasonably lucrative and most of the people had been charming, or, at the very least, pleasant. Not Megan.

'I didn't expect you to get so close to my face though,' Megan argued, pouting her enhanced lips at Abel, the weary, thirty-something director of the shoot.

'It's a head shot,' Bella argued. 'Where did you think I was going to put them?'

She had kept her temper in check until now, but everyone

was getting tired and Bella wasn't sure how much longer she could stand working with this prima donna.

Abel cleared his throat, interrupting her thoughts. 'I think we all need to take five minutes,' he said, quietly adding, 'Maybe grab a coffee, Bella, if you don't mind. I'd like a quick word with Megan.'

Bella did mind, she had a plane to catch. However, aware that arguing would only delay the shoot further, she nodded and walked away to the small room adjoining the studio where the refreshments had been laid out. She could hear Megan whining to Abel as she poured her coffee.

Bella had watched the reality series over the summer when Megan rapidly won the hearts of the viewers and couldn't believe that the girl she had thought so amusing on television was actually a complete cow. Bella wondered whose decision it had been on the production team to show Megan in a completely unrealistic light.

She had to hand it to the girl though, she was only twenty-two and her agent had already bagged her a book deal and various advertising deals. Now, after a drastic makeover, Megan needed new professional publicity shots, which required Bella's hands. Bella rubbed her throbbing temples with her fingertips. The novelty of the job had evaporated within an hour of working with her.

Her pocket vibrated. Wincing, she noticed that she had forgotten to change her settings to mute. She pulled her phone out of her jeans pocket, careful not to damage any of her nails. She went to switch it off before returning to the set, but spotting Jack's name on the display, glanced at the doorway and quickly answered his call.

'I have to be quick,' she whispered, placing her coffee on the nearby table. 'Abel will want me in a minute.'

'Lucky Abel,' he laughed.

Bella couldn't help smiling at the deep rumbling sound. 'Stop messing about. What do you want?'

'Are you back tonight?'

'I'm supposed to be, but Megan keeps causing delays. Why?'

'Sacha and Alessandro have invited us to try out a new soup she's thinking about serving at her café now it's autumn. I thought you might want to go, save either of us cooking.'

Bella smiled at the mention of her best friend, who also happened to be Jack's sister. She had never seen her so happy since she and Alessandro had got together a month before. 'Sounds good.'

'Shall I come and collect you from the airport?'

'That would be great,' she said, excited at the thought of seeing Jack. It wasn't easy hiding her feelings for him, especially as he rented one of the rooms at her boardwalk cottage, but it was something she had managed to do for years.

Hearing footsteps coming towards the canteen, she added, 'My plane gets in at about six tonight.'

'I'll see you then.'

She quickly ended the call and dropped her phone in her rucksack. Seconds later, Abel burst into the room, pushing the door with such force that it swung open and slammed against the wall.

'You okay?' she asked him, even though he clearly was anything but.

He took a deep breath and closed his eyes for a moment. 'That girl is impossible.'

She pulled a face. Looking forward to the meal at Sacha's café and an evening with Jack, she was past being polite. 'She is, but you have a shoot to complete and I have a plane to catch. So, shall we press on?'

Returning to Megan's side, Bella glanced at Abel. 'Do you want me to kneel next to her again, or do something else?' Like slap her, Bella thought, giving Megan a forced smile.

'Nah, the same as before,' Megan demanded. 'Just hurry the hell up, I'm meeting me fella in an hour.'

Delighted at this news, Bella knelt and twisted her body, reaching around Megan. She held her hand as lightly against the heavily made up face as she could, trying not to grimace.

It took another forty-five muscle aching minutes before Abel was satisfied with the shots the photographer had taken.

'Right, we're done,' Megan's agent cheered, holding up her faux fur coat for the girl to put on. Megan grunted a goodbye to the crew and marched out of the building. Bella couldn't help giggling at the collective sigh of relief that immediately followed her departure.

'I'll get going, too,' she said to Abel, fetching her coat and rucksack.

'Sorry about today,' he said, as she reached the exit. 'Give me a professional any time, most of them know how to behave.'

'It's fine,' Bella fibbed.

'Safe flight home.'

She smiled and raced out of the studio. The good thing about being a hand model was that she could wear what she liked to a shoot. It also meant being able to wear her favourite trainers, so her feet were always comfortable. She ran to the nearest underground station, smiling as she pictured her cosy cottage on the boardwalk, and Jack waiting for her to return.

2

'Alessandro? What are you doing here?' Bella tried to hide her disappointment as she left the departure hall at Jersey airport to find Alessandro waiting for her, instead of Jack.

'Jack, he have something he must do,' he said, looking, Bella thought, a little shifty.

She smiled at him and shook her head when he went to relieve her of her bag. Giving him a sideways glance as they walked outside towards the car park, she tried to imagine what had happened. Alessandro and Jack were her lodgers, so it wasn't as if she didn't spend time chatting to them both. For some reason though, Alessandro didn't seem to be his usual relaxed self. 'Is everything okay?'

He nodded. 'Yes.'

She didn't like to be ungrateful. After all, he had taken the time to come and collect her, so she didn't ask anything further about Jack's absence. The car doors made a clunking sound as the locks released. They got in and put on their seat belts.

'It was kind of you to come and get me,' she said, relieved to be on the island once again. 'Thanks.'

He smiled at her. 'Is fine.'

'Jack said something about a new soup Sacha's trying out,' she said, to break the awkward silence. 'I'm looking forward to it. It's been a long day and I'm starving, so I hope it's filling.'

Alessandro turned the key to start the engine and drove off. 'I'm to take you home,' he said. 'We will try the soup tomorrow, maybe.'

She was beginning to feel slightly concerned. 'Is everything okay with Sacha?'

'Yes, she is fine.' He gave her what Bella assumed was meant to be a reassuring smile.

Their plans had changed in the last couple of hours, so something must be amiss. What wasn't he telling her? 'Jack then?'

'He is at your cottage,' Alessandro answered after a little hesitation. 'Your day in London, it went well?'

It was obvious that he had no intention of telling her anything. She tried not to show how worried she felt at this turn of events. 'Not really, but it was good money and I'm back home again. I'm grateful that it's all over.'

To distract herself for the short journey, Bella told him about her day with Megan Knight.

Alessandro shook his head when she explained how rude the girl had been. 'And you say, she is only famous since last month?'

'I know,' she said, amused by his shock. 'Imagine what she's going to be like when she's had more attention from magazines and photographers.'

'You have to see her again?' he asked, indicating to turn into the car park near the boardwalk.

'No,' Bella said, relieved to be nearly home. 'Hopefully not.'

He parked, and they got out of the car. Breathing in the salty air, her mood lifted instantly. She had only been gone twelve hours, but it was heaven to be home. They crossed the road and made their way along the boardwalk to her blue painted cottage, The Bee Hive, halfway along.

The wind had picked up, she noticed. 'I've missed this place.'

'Is a good place to live,' he agreed, walking next to her. She liked Alessandro. He was always friendly and kind.

He had probably had a long day working at his *gelateria*, she thought, as they reached the front door. She grabbed hold of the doorknob, but before she could open it, the door lurched open pulling her with it. Yelling in shock, Bella flew inside and slammed face first into Jack's muscular chest.

'Oof.'

Jack grabbed hold of her arms, saving her dignity before she landed in a heap at his feet. 'Bloody hell, Bella! I didn't realise you were outside. You okay?'

Bella cleared her throat and pushed her long brown hair back from her crimson face. 'Um, yes.' She forced a smile. 'I'm fine.'

She kept forgetting that she had relaxed her rule about her lodgers having to enter the cottage by the back door, so that they could reach their room without going through the shop, which until Alessandro and Jack had moved in, was locked each night. She had felt it a necessity when strangers came to stay, but now, with two friends living with her it felt odd somehow to lock everything away. She'd also scrapped her rule of only giving them tea and biscuits laid out on a tray in each room. She wanted them to stay with her for as long as possible and making them feel as much at home as she could, would hopefully entice them to do so.

Realising he was going out, she asked, 'Where are you going in such a hurry?'

'Sorry I couldn't collect you, after all,' he said. 'Nicki's only gone and surprised me by flying over.' He frowned. 'She was on the phone giving me a mouthful and telling me she needed somewhere to stay, so Alessandro kindly went to meet you. I've got to fetch her from the airport now.'

Nicki, here, now? Hadn't they only split up a few weeks before?

'Where's she staying?' Bella asked, willing Jack not to ask if she could bunk up with him in his room. It was bad enough that she had a crush on him, without him getting back with his horrible girlfriend and her having to listen to them at night. She stepped further into the room, trying to look as if she wasn't fazed by this unwelcome news. 'Not here, I hope?'

'I've booked her a room at the Sea Breeze Hotel up the road. It was my first choice for when she was going to come over in the summer, but it was full then.'

Bella remembered. 'Are you looking forward to sorting things out with her?' She tried not to show how upsetting that would be for her.

'No.' Jack looked at her as if she was insane.

Bella couldn't help wondering why he was going to so much trouble when he clearly didn't want Nicki coming to the village. She decided that maybe he must really want to see her, after all.

'She's going to want to go over and over my reasons for breaking up with her, again.' The large ormolu clock on an art deco sideboard chimed the hour. Jack groaned. 'Hell, I'm going to be late. You sure you're okay?' Bella nodded. 'Right, better hurry. I don't need an argument as soon as she lands. I think there'll be more than enough of those without me giving her more fuel for her temper.'

Bella watched Jack run along the boardwalk towards the car park. He was so at home living near the beach, she hoped Nicki didn't guilt him in to returning with her to London and back to working in finance. She could barely imagine him going to work in a suit every day. When she pictured Jack, he was always wearing shorts. He had been like that ever since she'd known him when they were children.

The waves crashed against the granite sea wall, distracting her from her wistful thoughts. She loved living here with only the width of the boardwalk between her front door and the edge of the beach. She loved the drama of the tides, ebbing and flowing every twenty-four hours. She loved it best when it crashed against the wall, splashing over the boardwalk.

The spray from another wave drenched her. Bella licked the salty water from her lips and turned to go back inside. Shutting the door behind her, she took her bags straight upstairs and quickly showered and washed her hair. Then, once dried and dressed, she tied her hair up in a ponytail and followed her usual routine, slathering hand cream over her hands and fingers before pulling on one of her many pairs of cotton gloves to protect her skin and keep her nails as pristine as possible.

'Ah, you are wearing the pink gloves with the yellow stars today,' Alessandro teased, as he walked out of his bedroom.

Bella laughed. She was very fond of the handsome Italian, especially now that he and Sacha had sorted out the issue of their competing businesses, which had threatened to come between them. 'Yes, well I thought they would suit my mood.'

'You would like me to make you a cup of your tea?'

She smiled and nodded. Trust Alessandro to be the gentleman.

'How has your day been?' she asked. 'Still busy at the *gelateria*?'

'Yes, but not as busy as during the summer.' He disappeared into the kitchen returning moments later with a steaming mug of tea. 'Here you are,' he said, handing it to her.

They walked outside to the small yard behind her cottage.

'The sea's pretty rough this evening,' she said, as they sat at the distressed wooden table. 'I was thinking of extending out this way but I'm glad I didn't now.'

'It is a good place to have away from the... how you say... splash?'

She pictured the sea out the front of her home. 'The spray of the waves?'

'Yes, the spray. It is still warm enough to be outside.' He laughed. 'Nearly.'

Apart from when she was away from the island, Bella couldn't remember a day that she hadn't walked on the beach at some point. 'You're too used to Italian weather,' she joked. 'You'll soon toughen up after a winter here on the seafront.'

They sat in silence for a moment. Bella assumed that Alessandro's awkwardness earlier had been because Nicki was coming to stay. She didn't like to think that she was making anyone uncomfortable, especially about something that really was nothing to do with her. 'Alessandro,' she said. 'You don't have to be concerned about Nicki coming to Jersey you know.'

'She is not a very nice person, I think,' he said thoughtfully. 'Jack is your friend and also I know Sacha, she does not like Nicki.'

Bella took a sip of her drink. 'But it's up to Jack to decide what happens between them, not us.'

Alessandro nodded. 'Is true.'

She opened her mouth to speak only to be interrupted by a loud rapping on the heavy front door knocker. 'That sounds urgent,' she joked, putting down her mug and hurrying to answer the door.

The rapping was repeated.

'Hang on a sec,' she bellowed, irritated by the visitor's impatience.

She opened the door, pulling it back to be confronted by a wild-haired woman in her forties.

'Quick, let me in before I get soaked,' she said, pushing past Bella. 'You'd better close it unless you want to get wet too.'

Bella closed the door, trying to control her annoyance. 'Now, you listen here,' she began, turning to address the rude woman when she realised with a shock that it was her mother. 'Mum?'

Bella thought back to her childhood, living with her nan in this cottage. She barely remembered her mum, Claire, being at home but hadn't resented her absence. Even at ten she had been aware that living with Nan while her mum followed her dreams had been the right thing for her. She loved her mother, but as Nan explained often, her mum had barely been eighteen years old when Bella was born and was sorely lacking when it came to maternal feelings. 'Da, dah,' her mother sang, pulling Bella into a brief, awkward hug.

'Pleased to see me?'

She was, but her mother's arrival was usually followed by some form of disruption. 'Yes,' she said, taking her mother's worn leather jacket from her and hanging it on the back of one of her newly acquired mahogany carvers. 'Come through and meet Alessandro. He's one of my lodgers and we're having a drink out the back together.'

She led the way, trying not to feel concerned by this unexpected arrival. As they stepped outside, Alessandro stood up and looked from Bella to her mother. 'Good evening.'

She didn't blame him for looking confused. They were obviously related and could have passed for sisters. Bella recalled her nan giving her a brief lecture once when she complained that her mother didn't act like other mothers at school. 'If you're wanting a milk and cookies stay at home mum, Bella, then you're going to be disappointed. If you want to have a relationship with her, you need to accept her for who she is.'

That was part of Bella's problem though – she wasn't exactly sure who her mother was.

'This is my mum, Claire. Mum, this is Alessandro, Sacha's boyfriend.'

She cringed when her mum fluttered her eyelashes at him. 'Well, lucky Sacha,' she said as he stood up. She took his hand, pulling him towards her, kissing him on both cheeks. 'You're one of Bella's lodgers? I'm looking forward to meeting the other one now.'

'Yes,' Alessandro replied, looking stunned. 'You would like a drink?'

'Do you have gin?'

'We have wine,' Bella said. 'White, red and rosé, or tea or coffee.' She wondered how long her mother intended staying.

'Red for me.' She took a seat and dropped her small holdall at her feet. 'I can see you're wondering why I'm here,' she said, pinching Bella's cheek. 'Don't worry, it won't be for too long.'

Alessandro went to fetch Claire a glass of wine.

Bella picked up her mug and comforted herself by drinking.

'Which room have you put Alessandro in?'

'The large room at the front next to mine,' Bella said. 'Why?' She suspected that she knew the answer already.

'I'd rather have that room, but if it's occupied and he's paying rent, I suppose I'll manage with the smaller room at the back.'

Bella leant forward and lowered her voice. 'Mum, I said I have two tenants and there's only two bedrooms, so you can't stay here. You'll have to stay with one of your friends.'

Claire looked the picture of sadness. 'I'm your mother, Bella. I'd hoped you'd welcome me home.'

'Yes, but it would have been nice to have some warning, so

that I could make arrangements, don't you think?' Bella gritted her teeth, picturing Nan's kind face as she told her to hold her temper and not give her mother the satisfaction of playing the martyr. 'You haven't been back here for, what is it?' She tried to work out how many years had passed since her mother had bothered to come back to the boardwalk. 'Seven years?'

'Don't be ridiculous, it can't be that long.'

She could see that her mother knew exactly how long it had been and despite willing herself not to, Bella added, 'You didn't even come back for Nan's funeral.' She heard her voice crack with emotion.

It had been three years since her nan had died but it still hurt like hell. Some nights Bella would wake and think she heard her nan talking to her, upset to realise it was just a dream. Other times, usually when she had heard something funny, she thought how amused Nan would be when she repeated the story to her, only to remember that it was impossible and be upset.

Her mother reached out and placed a hand on Bella's arm. 'Sweetheart, there's not a day that goes by that I don't wish I could go back and rectify not being here for you.'

Bella wanted to believe her, but experience had taught her to know better. 'So why has it taken you another three years to make it back here then?'

'I'm here now,' she said, and smiled at Alessandro as he brought out her drink.

'Here you are.' Alessandro placed the glass of red wine on the table in front of Claire.

She looked suddenly downcast, and said to Bella, 'It's such a shame that you don't have room for me here. I was so looking forward to making it up to you for being away for so long. I suppose I'll have to go and book into the Prince of Wales, or the Sea Breeze Hotel, if they have space.'

Bella doubted her mother had the funds to do any such thing. She usually only came back when a relationship ended, and her money had run out. Bella knew as soon as Alessandro's smile disappeared that he was going to do the gentlemanly thing and offer his room to her mother.

'It's okay, Alessandro,' she implored, not looking forward to having her peaceful routine disrupted by her mother. 'Mum is happy to stay there. She'll only be down the road.'

He shook his head. 'No, this is not acceptable.'

Claire took her hand from Bella's arm and took hold of Alessandro, hugging him tightly. 'You charming, delightful man,' she said. 'Are you absolutely sure you won't mind?'

'Mum?' Bella stood up, knocking her mug over and spilling tea all over the table. 'Bugger.'

Alessandro looked mortified and shook his head. 'I insist. I am happy to stay there.' He stepped back from her mother. 'I will go now and ask if they have a room for me.'

Before Bella could argue, Alessandro left.

'You knew he'd do that, didn't you? You only want to stay here to save money. I rent the rooms out because I need the income, plus he's very nice. Bloody hell, Mum.'

Infuriated by her mother's self-satisfied smile, Bella had to try hard not to lose her temper completely. She walked through to the kitchen to fetch a cloth and mop up her spilt tea, removing her gloves and dropping them onto the worktop.

Alessandro returned a short while later. 'They have a room. I will take my things and go tonight. You can prepare the room for your mama.'

Claire got up, smiling at him, but before she could give him another hug, he side-stepped her and ran up the stairs.

Bella followed him. 'Really, you don't need to do this,' she said, reaching his bedroom door. 'Mum can share my bed. She doesn't need her own room.'

'No, I am happy to do this,' he reassured her. 'You and your mother need time to talk, I think.'

'You're not kidding, but I hate to feel like she's pushed you out.'

He shook his head. 'Please do not worry. When she has left I can come back again. Yes?'

'Yes,' Bella said miserably. 'I'll miss having you around though. It's been fun here with you and Jack, especially the evenings when Sacha calls in.' She thought of the times they'd laughed and drank until the small hours and how much she was going to miss them while her mother was staying.

Alessandro pulled a case from the wardrobe and filled it with a few of his clothes and shaving gear. 'It won't be for long maybe.'

She hoped not.

Bella left Alessandro in peace to pack his things. He soon joined her in the living room and she thanked him again as he left the cottage. Then turning to her mother, she said. 'Right, come and help me make up your room.'

She picked up her mother's holdall, unable to forget her manners. 'Follow me.'

They got to the room and her mother took her bag from Bella's grasp. 'I've only got a few things to hang up,' she said. 'I thought I could borrow some of your clothes if I needed to.'

Bella took a deep breath and walked to the airing cupboard to fetch some clean sheets and a towel. They stripped the bed and her mother helped her make it up again.

'Okay,' Bella said, grabbing the heap of bedlinen and towels she'd discarded on the floor. 'I'll take these downstairs to the washing machine and leave you to settle in for a bit.' And clear my mind before I completely lose it, she thought as she closed the bedroom door quietly and walked down the stairs.

Why, she wondered, did her mother have to return just when she was happy and settled for once? It had been a fun summer for the most part and that had been largely down to her two tenants. She hoped Jack wouldn't now decide to move out to join Alessandro at the hotel. After all, Nicki was staying there now, too. He might think it would make things easier all round.

She clicked open the door of the washing machine and pushed Alessandro's things inside. Setting the dial, she added the powder and slammed the door closed with more effort than she'd intended.

Jack. She tried to imagine how he was getting on but a vision of Nicki looking glamorous and perfectly made up came into her mind depressing her even further.

'Stop frowning,' her mother said, joining her in the kitchen. 'You'll get lines.'

Bella leaned back against the worktop and studied her mother in her skinny jeans, short glittery T-shirt and black biker boots. She was forty-eight, with the last thirty years of partying leaving only slight lines on her pretty face. She still thought she was twenty.

'Why have you really come back, Mum?'

3

'I thought you loved living in, where was it?' Bella asked, as they leaned against opposite wooden worktops in her galley kitchen.

'Mirissa,' Claire said, fiddling with the coloured glass beads on her bracelet.

'What about your boyfriend? Last time you wrote, you said you two were blissfully happy. Is he coming to stay, too?'

Claire shook her head. 'No. I've left him.'

Bella could see her mum was upset and her irritation towards her lessened. 'I'm sorry to hear that. What happened?'

'His vile mother never took to me,' she said quietly. 'She hated that he wanted to marry a woman who was...' she hesitated, glancing up at Bella. 'Well, I'm a year or more older than him. She was hoping he'd marry a younger girl and produce a large family.'

'How much older?' Bella asked. 'If you don't mind me asking.' Bella knew she would mind but wanted to be certain of all the details before she felt she could criticise the man's mother.

Claire shrugged. 'Twenty-one years.'

'So, that makes him twenty-seven. Mum, he's younger than I

am.' She couldn't help feeling slightly impressed. She liked the idea that her mother had enough confidence to date a man so much younger than her. 'I suppose I can see his mother's point of view though,' Bella admitted. 'But if he's happy then surely his mother shouldn't mind?' When her mother didn't reply, she added. 'Hang on, why are you here and not trying to make things work with him in Sri Lanka?'

Claire stood up. 'Because there are times, Bella, when you hope the man you love bloody stands up for you. I thought I'd get away from it all and come back here to catch up with you. While I'm away he can ponder on whether or not I'm going back.'

It made sense. 'Good for you. Well, I hope it all works out in the end.'

As annoying as her mother could be at times, Bella still hated seeing her upset. 'I'm sorry I wasn't a bit more welcoming,' she said. 'It's been a trying day. I know that's no excuse, but you caught me off guard.'

'That's all right. Can I have a hug now? A proper one, mind.'

Bella smiled and stepped into her mother's outstretched arms, breathing in the familiar patchouli-based scent she always associated with her. She couldn't help wondering how long it would be until her mother became bored of life on the boardwalk and yearn to return to Sri Lanka. She just hoped she didn't get too used to her being back, only to be devastated when she suddenly announced her departure, as was usually the case.

The front door closed, alerting her to Jack's return.

'Bella?' he bellowed. 'Fancy a quickie?'

She froze, stepping back from her giggling mother.

'He means a drink,' she whispered through clenched teeth. 'Through here, Jack.'

She could hear his heavy footsteps as he neared the kitchen.

'Well, look who it is,' he beamed, recognising Claire. 'The happy wanderer returns.'

Bella's heart contracted watching his handsome tanned face as he kissed her mother on the cheek. 'You're looking amazing, Claire.'

'She does, doesn't she?' Bella said. 'But she's kicked poor Alessandro out of his bedroom.'

'He offered,' Claire nudged her in the ribs. 'You make it sound as if I insisted.'

Bella pulled a face at Jack. 'Put it this way, he's too much of a gentleman not to offer.'

'So that's why I saw him at the Sea Breeze?' Jack said, enlightened by this news.

'You didn't speak to him?'

Jack sighed heavily. 'Too busy listening to Nicki's speech to be able to chat with anyone else.'

Bella pictured Jack's sleek ex cornering him. He was a free spirit and she still couldn't imagine what had attracted them to each other in the first place. 'Didn't go too well then?'

'She still insists that we should give it another go, despite me telling her that I have no intention of returning to the mainland.' He walked into the kitchen. 'Drinks, anyone? I know I need one.'

Bella couldn't help smiling at this news. Jack was happiest on the beach. When he wasn't helping Sacha run the café he was surfing, or rock climbing. She doubted he could stand living in a city for too long. 'Surely she doesn't expect you to go back and live in London, not really?'

'She does,' he said, reaching into the fridge and taking out three bottles of lager. 'Claire?'

Bella watched her mother take her drink and then, taking one from Jack, followed her into the living room and sat down. 'Sacha will be glad that you've decided to stay here.'

Jack took a mouthful from his bottle. 'Not really. She's already told me that she'll be reducing the opening hours for the café in the next two weeks. She wants to keep young Milo on for Saturdays, which is great, but there's no point keeping it open when fewer people come to the boardwalk now summer's over.'

'I'm sure you'll find something though?' She tried to come up with a suggestion.

'We'll see.' He stared into the cold fireplace. 'I was offered work by Tony Le Quesne this morning when he overheard me and Sacha chatting.'

'Who?' Claire asked.

'He's a fisherman who moors his boat down here,' Bella explained. 'He's a widower, sadly. He has two small children.'

Jack added, 'His wife died a while back. Must be eighteen months or so now. He's finding it a bit difficult without her, poor bloke.'

Bella pictured the handsome man who took his children to eat at the café most days. Sacha had spoken about him many times. Bella had seen him several times too and he always looked as if he was trying to put on a happy face for his children's sakes. 'I gather from Sacha that he and his wife were very much in love.'

'Poor sod.'

They fell silent, each lost in their own thoughts. Bella wondered if there was ever a time when a bereft person could truly move on from losing the love of their life. She sighed miserably. Would she ever find a love that strong? She hoped so.

'Hey,' Jack said, making Bella and Claire jump. 'Enough wallowing. How about I treat you ladies to a bite to eat at Summer Sundaes? You must be famished if you've only just arrived, Claire?'

The words were barely out of his mouth when Bella remembered that she had been supposed to go there to try Sacha's new soup with him.

'That would be perfect,' her mother said. Never one to miss an opportunity, she finished her drink within seconds and, standing up, linked her arm through Jack's. 'Come along, Bella, before he changes his mind.'

Jack ruffled Bella's hair. 'Bella knows that when food is on my mind I'm not easily distracted.'

'I do?' Bella smiled, putting down her half-empty bottle. She got up and, pulling on her puffy jacket, followed her mother and Jack outside and locked the door. She walked behind them as Claire chatted to Jack, almost slamming into the back of him when he suddenly stopped.

'Come on,' he said, putting his free arm out for her to take. 'Let's get a move on. We don't want to get there after closing time.'

Sacha was standing at the café window, her arms folded across her chest, staring out to sea thoughtfully when they arrived.

'You okay, Sis?' Jack asked, leading Bella and Claire to a nearby table.

'Hi,' Sacha said, eyes widening as she spotted Claire. She rushed over to give her a hug. 'When did you get back? Bella didn't tell me you were coming home.'

Bella pulled out a chair and sat down. 'That's because Bella didn't know either,' she joked.

Sacha frowned. 'Where are you staying? Prince of Wales? Sea Breeze Hotel?'

'Never mind that.' Jack motioned for her to be quiet. 'I'll explain everything while Claire and Bella decide what they're going to eat,' he said, leading her away to the counter.

Bella didn't have to look at the menu, she knew its contents by heart. 'I was wondering if you wanted us to try your new soup?'

Sacha shook her head. 'No, don't worry. I've decided I need to tweak the recipe just a little, though I've yet to decide exactly how.'

She chose a tuna and cheese toasted sandwich and glanced at Jack, assuming he was explaining about Alessandro giving up his room for Claire. He always tried to be the peace-keeper if he thought there was going to be an argument. She was grateful to him. She didn't want to be angry with her mother. She really was happy to see her again, but knew her well enough to be aware that with her mother came drama. She just hoped that this time things would be different.

* * *

They finished their meal and Bella wiped her mouth on her napkin, surreptitiously watching her mother doing the same. Her heart swelled with love for the woman who had spent little time with her growing up, but who livened things up whenever she was around. She noticed her mother's attention had wandered and followed her gaze out of the window onto the boardwalk. Seeing nothing, she asked, 'Everything okay?'

Claire squinted and peered into the darkness, lit only by the café's interior lights now that the coloured bulbs, strung from lamp post to lamp post during the summer, had been taken down for the winter.

'I was sure I saw someone walking along out there.'

'I didn't see anything,' Bella said, scanning the area. 'I doubt anyone will be strolling along the boardwalk tonight, not with the storm forecast later. Was it one of my neighbours?'

'No idea. Probably my overactive imagination.' Claire looked unconvinced by her own words.

'Does it feel strange to be back here again?'

Her mother looked thoughtful for a moment as she ate the last mouthful of fish from her plate. Setting her knife and fork down at twenty-five-past four, like Bella recalled her Nan insisting she always did at the end of her meal, Claire eventually said, 'It always feels a little strange coming back. It's like stepping into a childhood memory, a bit like entering a protected bubble. It always revives my spirit to spend time here.'

Bella liked her mother's sentiment and wondered why she didn't return more often. 'I'm glad.'

They finished their drinks and after arguing briefly with Sacha about paying for their food, prepared to leave.

'You can come and help me set up in here for the Halloween party I'm giving for the boardwalk locals early on Friday evening before the children go out trick or treating,' Sacha suggested, as Bella helped her clear their plates.

'It's a deal,' Bella said, following Sacha to the kitchen.

'Leave these, I'll sort them out.'

They rejoined the others in the café just as spray covered the window.

Claire gasped. 'It really is getting nasty out there tonight.'

'And it's just gone high tide.' Jack grabbed hold of their jackets. 'If you're okay for us to leave, Sacha, we'd better get back to the cottage before we all get swept away.'

Sacha put down the plates and followed them to the door. 'Please pull down the metal shutters for me, Jack, I don't want any broken windows.'

'No problem.' He turned to Bella and Claire. 'If you wait a sec, I'll close the shutters. Sacha doesn't need any pebbles shattering the windows.'

'I'll do that with you,' Bella said, pulling on her gloves. 'You go up and close the ones over your upstairs windows.'

'Will do,' Sacha said. 'Then you must go and do the same at your cottage.'

Jack opened the door, holding it tightly as he and Bella went outside.

What a difference from a month ago when the summer was still in force and storms meant thunder and lightning, without this chilly wind, Bella thought, grabbing one of the shutters and pulling it closed so that Jack could fasten the catch.

They went back inside.

'I didn't realise it was going to be so bad,' Claire said, zipping up the cloth jacket that Bella reasoned wouldn't keep out a shower, let alone a storm and sea spray.

Bella saw Sacha had begun cashing up her till. 'You'll be okay tonight?'

Sacha looked up. 'As soon as you three have left I'll lock up and go to bed. I love hearing storms from inside my flat, especially if I know everything is secure down here.'

'Right, if you're okay for us to leave,' Jack said, staring out of the window with concern. 'We'd better get going.'

Sacha gave each of them a hug. 'Thanks for coming. Now, go home before it gets even more dangerous out there. This wind is getting stronger by the minute.'

Jack held the door open, waiting for Sacha to lock it behind them. Then, taking Bella and Claire by the hand, the three of them hurried along the boardwalk. The wind almost took Bella's breath away. She tucked her chin and mouth into the neck of her jacket, blinking back the sandy spray of the incoming tide. It was stupid of them to venture out on such a night, she reasoned, shivering as she jogged to keep up with Jack's large strides. They could be hit by debris from the waves at any point.

She heard her mother yelp and Jack's concerned tone as he checked that she was okay before pulling them onward once again towards the cottage.

Within two minutes they were home. Bella fumbled in her pocket for the key and unlocked the front door. As she turned the handle, a strong gust of wind forced the heavy door open, smashing it against the wall inside her living room.

'Go in,' she shouted. 'I'll quickly close the shutters.'

'No, you stay in here,' Jack said, pulling her inside the cottage. 'I'll do it.'

'I can manage perfectly well,' she argued, indignant that he thought she might be incapable.

'Both of you can do the bloody shutters,' Claire shouted, windswept and wet from their walk. 'Just get a move on, you're letting all the rain and cold in here.'

Jack hurried to the furthest window and carefully undid the metal clasps holding each shutter back, before making sure they were firmly secured. Secretly relieved he was saving her time by helping, Bella did the same with the window closest to the door. He waited for her to walk ahead of him and when they were both inside they took off their dripping coats.

'I must look such a mess?' Claire asked, brushing her messy hair and tying it back in a band.

'I think we all probably do,' Bella said. 'I'll light the fire and get some heat into this room.'

She walked over to the small wood burner and bent down. Reaching out for some newspaper to screw up to help to get the flames going, she heard Jack zipping up a dry, hooded jacket.

'Where are you going?'

'Betty,' he said, his face taut with concern. 'I need to check on her and see if she's okay.'

She couldn't believe that she hadn't thought of doing the

same. Bella always checked on the oldest resident on the boardwalk. Or, if she was away, one of the other locals called in on her to ensure everything was secure and she had all that she needed.

'Shall I come with you?' she offered guiltily.

'No.' He shook his head. 'You set that up. I shouldn't be too long.'

'If you're not back in fifteen minutes I'll know something is wrong and will come down to find you.'

Jack shook his head. 'Stop panicking, Bella. Betty has a phone and I'll ring you if I need to. Now, you concentrate on setting that fire and I suggest you change into something warm. You're soaked through.'

Bella took off her jacket and held out her hand waiting to take her mother's.

Their wet hair and soaked clothes clung to their bodies and she noticed her mother's teeth chattering. She took the jackets and hung them in the small boiler room at the back of the kitchen. Then, coming back into the living room, Bella drew the curtains.

'I don't know why you're bothering to do that,' Claire said, frowning. 'It's already dark in here.'

'It makes it feel cosier though, don't you think?'

'I suppose so.'

'You look frozen, Mum,' she said. 'Why not go upstairs, take a hot shower and change into something dry? By the time you get back down here, this room should have heated up a bit. I'll do the same and then I can make us a couple of hot milky drinks.'

'Sounds wonderful,' Claire said, rubbing her arms.

Bella watched as her mother left the room. She looked even more petite than Bella recalled. Then again, her mother had such luscious wild curls, and always wore floaty skirts and tops so that it was difficult to decipher her exact size.

Seconds later Claire shouted down from the upstairs landing. 'Do you mind if I borrow something of yours to wear?'

'No,' Bella replied, trying to think what best to suggest. 'You'll find several tracksuits in the large cupboard in my bedroom. Help yourself.'

She could hear her mother's footsteps as she walked across the creaking bedroom floorboards, amused to imagine her looking through the clothes in her cupboard and discarding most of them as too tatty. Bella screwed up a couple of pages of the local newspaper and pushed them into the wood burner, then placing a few pieces of kindling and a couple of pressed lighters she had bought from the nearest garage, set about lighting it. She heard the light click on in the upstairs bathroom and then the water in the shower splashing against the tiles.

Too cold to wait for the fire to get going, she went into the small galley kitchen, half-filled a saucepan with milk and placed it on the Aga to heat for their drinks.

She heard the bathroom door open. 'All yours, lovey,' Claire shouted before her footsteps could be heard running along the short corridor and into her bedroom.

Bella ran up to the bathroom and locked the door. Peeling off each of her items of clothing, she let them land on the floor in a wet puddle. Bella was glad of the steaminess of the usually cold bathroom as it made the room pleasantly warm. She turned on the shower and stepped in, sighing when the heat of the water coursed over her, instantly warming her.

After washing her hair, she stepped out of the shower and wrapped a towel around her wavy dark hair, before drying herself with a larger fluffy towel. She tidied up the room so that it was ready for Jack to shower when he returned and, bracing herself for the cool of the corridor, opened the door and ran to her room.

Dressed, and with her hair roughly dried and tied up in a ponytail, Bella hurried downstairs to check on the milk. She reached the kitchen in time to see the milk boiling and rising up the sides of the pan. Only just managing to rescue it before it overflowed, she quickly placed it on the back of the Aga to cool slightly and took out three mugs. She was spooning powdered hot chocolate into the third mug when Jack made a noisy entrance.

'It's Baltic out there,' he said, shaking his head and sending droplets around him in an arc. 'Betty's fine though. I said I'd call on her at nine-thirty tomorrow morning and treat her to breakfast at Summer Sundaes. You and your mum are welcome to join us.'

Bella concentrated on pouring the hot milk carefully into the three mugs and stirring the liquid. There was just enough, she was relieved to note.

'Glad to know Betty's okay,' she said. 'Mentally she's very tough, but I suspect she hides her frailties from us a bit.'

'I agree.' He took off his jacket.

'Give that to me,' she said, taking the dripping article. As she lifted it to hang it on a peg near the boiler, rivulets of water ran up her sleeve. 'Yuck.'

'Sorry about that.'

She laughed and shook her arm. 'Fine. I've made us all a hot chocolate, so if you want to jump in the shower quickly while it cools a bit, then we can all sit down by the fire.'

'Perfect,' he said, giving her a smile that made her heart melt and face redden.

Seeing he was oblivious to the reaction, Bella added, 'Give Mum a call when you get upstairs, will you? Ask her to come down to the living room.'

'Will do.'

Bella took the drinks and placed them on an antique oak table near the fire. She added a couple of logs to keep the fire at its peak, ready for her mum and Jack to join her. Switching off the overhead light, she clicked on two table lamps, satisfied with the warm glow they gave the room, despite the howling wind outside.

Sitting down, Bella picked up her mug and cupped it in her hands, breathing in the milky chocolaty scent of her drink, and listened to the waves crashing against the sea wall, and pebbles hitting the shuttered windows. She loved stormy nights like these, but only when she was warm and cosy inside her cottage. She couldn't help feeling sorry for Alessandro, aware how much he would have enjoyed being with them, rather than in a hotel with strangers.

Thinking of the hotel, her mind wandered to Nicki. Would she become friendly with Alessandro? Knowing what she did about Nicki, she wouldn't put it past her to spend her time working on Alessandro until she found out all she could about Sacha and her café. From what she knew of Nicki, the woman wouldn't hesitate to use any underhand tactics to keep Jack from staying on the island.

When Claire joined her, Bella laughed at how baggy her tracksuit was on her mum. 'I didn't realise I was taller than you by that much,' she giggled as Claire sat down. 'You've even had to roll up the bottoms.'

'Yes, several times, and the sleeves.'

She was also wearing Bella's favourite fluffy bed socks. Bella didn't mind. In fact, it was heart-warming to see her mother dressed in the fleecy tracksuit and looking so relaxed.

'This is yours,' she said when Claire had made herself comfortable on the chair nearest the fire. She handed her mum a mug and watched her breathe in the delicious scent, just as she had moments before.

'Hot chocolate,' Claire beamed. 'I haven't had this since the last time I stayed here when your nan was alive. Do you remember?'

Bella allowed herself to think back to a particularly freezing March when snowdrifts had blocked the roads, stopping Claire's flight from leaving the island. She cleared her throat, determined not to get emotional at the memory. 'I do. I remember you panicking that you'd miss your connecting flight when your plane was grounded.'

Claire laughed. 'I couldn't even get to the airport, so I don't know why I was so bothered about the plane taking off.'

Each lost in thought for a few seconds, they then smiled at each other. 'Your nan loved nights like these,' Claire reminisced.

'She did.'

'One of those mine?' Jack asked, breaking their sentimental thoughts.

'I didn't see you there,' Bella said, glad for the interruption before she gave in to her still present grief. She handed him his mug. 'Take a seat.'

He sat down in the middle chair facing the fire, stretching his long legs out in front of him, his feet only inches from the metal log burner. 'This is perfect.' He took a tentative sip of his drink. 'I don't often drink hot chocolate, but this makes me wonder why the hell not.'

Bella laughed. 'Probably because you're too lazy to make it.'

'Or,' Claire added. 'Because you only think as far as a bottle of beer.'

'Hey, steady on, you two. No ganging up. Anyway, that's not true.' He grinned.

'Okay,' Claire said, shuffling her bum to sit up straighter in her chair. 'Tell me, when exactly was the last,' she winked at Bella. 'Or even the first time you made hot chocolate?'

Jack contemplated his answer, taking a few sips of his drink as he did so to keep them waiting. 'Fine. I don't think I've ever made it, but I will do from now on, that's for sure.'

Bella doubted it. 'I look forward to tasting your efforts,' she said. She closed her eyes for a moment, warmed by the heat of the log burner and being in the company of Jack and her mum. It was an unexpected treat.

'I'm a little peckish,' Jack said, sitting upright.

'We only ate an hour ago,' Bella laughed, unsure whether or not she was ready to eat more food.

'Anyone want to join me in a few rounds of hot buttered toast? I bought a cabbage loaf from Sacha earlier today,' he added unnecessarily.

'I dream of cabbage loaf when I'm in Sri Lanka,' Claire said. 'Only one piece for me though, thanks.'

'Do you want any help?' Bella asked, relishing the thought of her favourite snack.

'Nope,' Jack said, finishing his drink and standing up. 'You two stay here.'

Claire and Bella looked at each other and nodded. 'Fine by us,' Bella said.

She and Claire sat sipping their drinks, listening to Jack opening and closing drawers and cupboards in the kitchen as he searched for knives, plates and butter. Soon the tantalising smell of toasted cabbage loaf emanated from the kitchen and Jack appeared, carrying three plates of perfectly toasted slices the size of small doorsteps.

'Now that is what I call a treat,' Claire laughed when he handed her a plate with a huge slice of toast dripping with Jersey butter. 'And served by such a handsome waiter.'

'Get your neck around that,' he laughed. 'Then tell me I'm not the best toast chef in the business.'

Bella shook her head. 'Big head,' she teased, taking her plate and biting greedily into the huge slab of toast in her hand. She chewed and swallowed the delicious confection. 'Yes, you are now officially King of the Toasted Cabbage Loaf. Better get used to making it for us.'

He gave a slight bow before sitting down and eating. Groaning in pleasure, he swallowed a mouthful. 'I missed this stuff when I was living away too, Claire. This is my favourite bread of all time.'

Bella couldn't help being amused by his rapture. She looked across at her mum who had a similar expression on her face as she ate in silence, relishing every mouthful.

'Perfection,' Claire said eventually.

When they had finished, Bella cleared away the plates and joined them in the living room. 'Why don't you tell us a little about Jayvani, Mum. I don't know much about your life in Sri Lanka.'

'I've never been but I've always wanted to go,' Jack said. 'Nicki hated the thought, but now we're no longer together there's nothing to hold me back.'

Bella briefly pictured accompanying Jack on his travels.

'You've never come to visit either, Bella,' Claire said with a hint of accusation. 'You really should make the effort.' She stared at the flames dancing wildly in the fireplace for a moment. 'We could show you around. I'm sure you'd fall in love with the place.'

'I'd love to,' Bella admitted. 'But I'd have to find someone to look after the shop while I was away, or close it, and I couldn't leave the cottage with lodgers staying here.'

'You could make some sort of plan though,' Claire said, a hopeful tone in her voice.

'Yes,' Bella agreed, not sure how she would manage it. 'I'd need to save to come. I don't have any spare cash at the moment.' She didn't ever have any spare cash, but didn't need to let her mum know that. She didn't want Claire to worry about her unnecessarily.

'You have a decent amount of antiques here, Bella,' her mother said, looking around the room. 'Surely if you make a concerted effort you could sell a few and make some money?'

'Essentially, that's true,' she agreed, stroking the wide arms of the forties chair, enjoying their softness. 'But this is a quiet time for sales. Hopefully, I should get a few closer to Christmas.'

They descended into a comfortable silence, each lost in their own thoughts.

'We need a party,' Jack announced. Claire stared at him, looking happy at the thought.

'Really?' Bella asked, listening to a thunder clap. The last thing she felt like doing was having to trek out in the cold to a party. She was happy at home. 'I'm happy with a good book and hibernating in front of the fire until spring.'

'At your age I never turned down the offer of a party,' Claire said.

Bella resisted looking at her. She doubted her mother's party lifestyle had changed much since she was in her late twenties. 'Why, though?' she asked, waiting for Jack to answer.

'Because it's nearly Halloween and it'll be fun.'

'I'd rather celebrate bonfire night,' Claire said. 'I get spooked by all those ghouls and ghosts.'

'I suppose Halloween isn't too bad, but I'm not so sure about bonfire night,' Bella said, thinking of Mrs Jones' little terrier, Teddy. 'I worry about the animals around here and how terrified they're made by noisy fireworks. Anyway, don't forget Sacha is organising something for Halloween for the locals, before the kids go trick or treating.'

Claire nodded. 'She has a point, Jack.'

Jack slapped his hands down on the arms of his chair and grinned. 'Why don't we source noise-free fireworks for the fifth then?'

Was there such a thing? 'Do they exist, or are they something you've imagined?'

He pulled a face at her. 'I wish I had thought them up, I might have made some money out of the idea. No, they are a reality. What do you think? If we get them, no one can complain. Babies and pets won't be frightened, and we don't have to feel guilty.'

Bella mulled over his words. 'Well, if you can get them then I'd be up for it,' she said, unable to resist his enthusiasm for the idea. 'Where would we have the bonfire?'

'The beach.' Jack looked delighted at his suggestion.

Bella wriggled her toes in front of the fire. 'But what about high tide twice every day. How do you suggest getting around that?'

'Let me think about it.' He rubbed his chin.

Bella watched his long, tanned fingers grazing lightly over his stubble. How could being messy make Jack seem even more attractive to her? 'I'm sure you'll come up with something, you usually do.'

'What was the best bonfire night you remember?' Claire asked.

They had a good think.

'Probably when I was a kid and my dad took Sacha and me to a massive bonfire party at a farm somewhere in St Peter's,' Jack said, smiling. 'Not sure where it was now though. You?'

'I'm trying to choose,' Claire said. 'When I was young we had smaller family parties with a few Catherine wheels, rockets and sparklers. Dad was alive then and we usually went to one of his work colleagues' homes. I remember the smell as they served hot dogs for the children, while the adults ate plates of curry and drank mulled wine.'

'It sounds fun,' Bella said, enjoying hearing her mother reminisce.

'It was. The funniest I recall was when it was foggy and us children could only see a glimmer of a firework in the distance, and the dads were shouting at us from the end of the garden to concentrate and look at the misty display.'

Bella and Jack laughed at her memory.

'We'll do something. Get everyone from the boardwalk involved and each of us can either prepare food, drink or something to do with the fireworks. What do you say?'

'I think it would be fun,' Bella said honestly. 'It's good to have things going on at this time of year, otherwise it's too quiet,' she said, warming to the idea. 'It's always a little too quiet on the boardwalk after the noise and excitement of summer.'

'Then it's agreed,' he said enthusiastically. 'I'll come up with a plan. We can chat about it tomorrow after I've seen Sacha and Betty at the café and find out what they have to say about it. You two can join us for breakfast too, if you want?'

'I'd love to.' Claire smiled at Bella. 'What about you?'

'I won't, thanks. I've got too much to do here. You can fill me in when you get back though,' Bella said, excited at the prospect. 'Now, I'd better get started with a manicure before I'm too tired to bother.'

'Now?' Claire asked. 'Your hands look perfect to me.'

Bella was used to people commenting on her hands and how perfect they were, but to her they were tools of her part-time money earner and needed constant care. 'Thank you, but I never know when I'm going to be contacted for a shoot and need them to be immaculate at all times.'

'She's the only person I know who has to wear gloves for most of the summer,' Jack said, glancing at Bella's hands. 'I would have no idea how much work it takes to keep them looking so good if I didn't live here.'

Her mum looked astonished. 'Well, who knew you could make a living from having your hands photographed. Serves me right for not keeping in better contact with you, Bella. It seems there's a lot about you that I've yet to learn.'

Bella shrugged. 'Likewise.'

She was part way through oiling her right hand when there was a knock at the door. She looked at the wall clock and noticed it was nearly eleven. 'Who can that be at this time?'

'I'll go and see,' Jack said, getting up from his chair and answering the door. 'It could be some nutter.'

4

Bella and Claire sat in silence, waiting to hear who had called at the cottage so late.

During Bella's lifetime living here, there had been the odd local who had caused a stir with their eccentric ways, and one or two holidaymakers giving the residents of the boardwalk reason to widen their eyes in shock, but no one who had ever made her feel threatened in any way. She smiled at the thought of an ex-circus owner who had attempted to train her nan's elderly Border collie years before. He'd been given a nip for his efforts and then a stern telling off from her nan when he had dared to complain about the dog.

'What's the matter, Tony?' she heard Jack ask. He was holding tightly to the door, so it wouldn't bang against the wall in the strong winds.

Bella mouthed the word 'fisherman' to her mother when Claire gave her a questioning look.

'I'm glad you're in, Jack,' Tony said, sounding exhausted. 'I've been tying up several of the boats, checking their moorings. I'm having a little difficulty with my own boat though. Could you spare half an hour to help me?'

'Not a problem, mate,' Jack said. He looked over his shoulder at Bella as he grabbed his jacket. 'I won't be long, I'm just going to help Tony,' he shouted unnecessarily.

'Be careful,' Claire shouted back. 'It's fierce out there tonight.'

Bella finished working on her hands. Concerned for Jack, she picked up their mugs and took them to the kitchen. She wished now that the shutters weren't blocking her view of the small harbour.

'I hope they're alright,' she said, filling the sink. She pulled on her favourite pink washing-up gloves, with purple faux marabou feathers around the wrists, which Sacha had bought her last Christmas, and began washing up the mugs.

'He'll be fine,' Claire said, coming up behind her. 'You like him, don't you?'

'What a thing to say.' Bella blushed. She wasn't used to having someone around who could read her so well. And she especially didn't need her mother putting her foot in it and saying the wrong thing to Jack when he got back. 'I don't,' she fibbed. When her mother went to argue, Bella raised her hand. 'Fine. But please, don't speak to him about it, or make insinuations. If you do, you'll have to go and stay at the pub.'

Claire threw her head back, laughing. 'You're such a drama queen. When have I ever said the wrong thing?'

Bella stared at her mother in astonishment. Didn't she know herself at all? Hands on her hips, she said, 'I couldn't count the times you've done exactly that,' she said, trying to listen out for Jack coming back. She couldn't bear him to arrive home and overhear this conversation. 'And I wouldn't mind if it was unintentional but we both know that each time you happened to share information, you knew exactly what you were doing. You just can't help yourself.'

'Cheek.' Claire pulled a shocked face. She wrapped her skinny arms around Bella's shoulders and hugged her. 'You know I love you, don't you?'

'Yes,' Bella admitted, soothed slightly by the reminder. 'But we're not debating that, are we?'

'I know.' Claire let go and stepped back, resting her bottom against the opposite worktop. 'But I've barely been around while you've been growing up and now, it's odd seeing you as a capable woman in your late twenties.' She smiled. 'In fact, it makes me feel quite old, I can tell you.'

Bella shook her head, recalling how much her mother worried about her age. She'd never known her to be honest about how old she was and certainly never introduced Bella as her own daughter on the odd occasion they had gone out together on the island.

'Mum, when are you going to stop fussing about how old you are?'

'You're young, it's easy for you.' Claire sighed heavily.

'Don't pull that act on me,' Bella said, flicking bubbles from the sink at her. 'Nan told me that when you were eighteen you pretended you were older. Then when you hit twenty-five you lied about your age and wanted people to think you were younger.' She thought for a moment. 'How old does your boyfriend think you are?'

'I don't know,' her mother answered, irritated for once. 'Anyway, what he doesn't know won't hurt him as long as he loves me.' She pointed at Bella. 'Which he does.'

Bella couldn't help saying, 'Good. But if you're both so happy together why are you here and not in Sri Lanka with him?' Claire went to answer, but Bella interrupted her. 'And don't try to say that you needed to see me, because we both know that you never visit purely to catch up with me, but usually because you're running away from something else in your life.'

She hoped she didn't sound bitter, because she certainly didn't feel that way. She was simply stating a fact. Her nan had always been straight about her mother's actions, telling Bella often how loved and cared for she was, and she'd had no reason to wallow. Consequently, she had never felt sorry for herself growing up.

'Look,' Bella added, trying to soften her previously harsh words. 'Don't get me wrong, I'm thrilled you're here. I love spending time with you, but I know how you put on a brave face and I simply don't believe there's nothing wrong. So,' she narrowed her eyes. 'What's the problem this time, Mum?'

Claire thought for a moment. She seemed conflicted about something, but eventually said, 'I love Jayvani and want him to commit, but he's being influenced by that cow of a mother of his.'

Now, she was getting somewhere. 'If he loved you as much as you say then surely he won't care what his mother thinks.'

Claire shook her head sadly. 'It's not like that. As much as I love him, and I do, he's turned out to be just like all the other men I've known: soft when it comes to his mother.'

Bella could see that Claire was genuinely upset, and felt mean for delving into her private life. 'It's fine,' she said. 'If he doesn't love you enough to come after you, or find a way to persuade you to go back to him, then he's the one who'll lose out.' And the idiot, she thought, thinking how much fun her mum always was.

A large wave sent several pebbles crashing against the shutters making them jump. Bella couldn't help worrying about Jack.

'He's a strapping lad and knows the sea well,' her mother said, sensing her concern. 'He won't do anything reckless and I'm sure he'll be home soon.'

Bella hoped she was right.

5

They stayed up chatting for two more hours, but there still wasn't any sign of Jack. Bella checked her phone in case she'd missed a text from him and then her watch.

'Stop doing that,' Claire said. 'He'll be back when he's finished helping the fisherman.'

Bella sighed. Her mother was right. She was shattered and sitting here fretting wasn't going to bring Jack home any sooner. She covered her mouth as she yawned. 'You're right. I'm going to have to get some sleep,' she said. 'I've got to prepare for the Autumn Market I'm taking part in over the weekend.'

'I'm exhausted, too. Let's get to our beds.'

Bella closed the wood burner doors, and leaving one light on for Jack when he got back, followed her mother upstairs.

'I hope he's home soon though,' she said, turning to her mother as she reached her bedroom door. She tried to stay calm, but was unable to push aside her anxiety. 'What if something's happened to them? Would we know?'

'That Tony chap will no doubt have a radio on his fishing boat, and anyway, they're only in the harbour.'

'Then, what's taking them so long?' Bella asked, aware her voice was rising. It wasn't fair to snap at her mother, she realised, embarrassed. 'Sorry. I'll go to bed now.'

Claire walked over to her and gave her a hug. 'Get some sleep. I'm sure everything will be fine in the morning.'

'Yes, you're probably right,' Bella said, hugging her back. 'Good night.'

* * *

After failing to fall asleep until the early hours, fretting about Jack's absence, Bella woke later than she'd intended the following morning. She stared bleary-eyed at her alarm clock for a few seconds, unsure whether she'd inadvertently pressed snooze, or forgotten to set it in the first place. She listened out for the wind, relieved that it had died down and that the storm seemed to have passed.

She lay in bed, listening to see if she could hear him making a noise somewhere in the cottage, and smiled as his deep voice sang the wrong words to a tune on the radio in the kitchen.

Looking forward to seeing him, she stretched and flung back her thick duvet. She stepped out of her bed onto the blue and yellow, moon and stars rag rug her nan had made her when she was little and pushed her feet in to her slippers. It was never usually this cold in mid-October, she mused, grabbing her fleecy dressing gown from the end of her bed.

She hoped the weather would warm up a bit before the winter months really did kick in. Bright sunshine shone through her thin flowery curtains. She narrowed her eyes as she pulled them aside to let them become accustomed to the light, then peered out over the boardwalk to the sea. She could see pebbles and some driftwood scattered around, but the sea was still, like a village pond. She wasn't surprised as this often happened after an especially stormy night. She remembered her nan telling her that holidaymakers were often taken aback by this extreme change in the weather over the course of only a few hours, but it was something she had experienced many times.

Moving away from the window, Bella looked at her reflection in her dressing table mirror and groaned. 'I look like a dishevelled octogenarian,' she murmured, brushing her hair and trying to force her curls in to some semblance of tidiness. It didn't work, so she tied her hair in a ponytail and went to the bathroom to wash her face and clean her teeth.

Jack sang louder as he clattered about in the kitchen. How was he always such an early riser? she wondered, smiling. He never seemed to oversleep and was always cheerful in the mornings. She wished she could be a little more like him in that respect.

She went downstairs to join him. 'Morning, cheerful,' she said, watching him butter his toast and wash up his knife afterwards.

He picked up his mug of tea and plate, giving her a wide smile. 'Good morning to you. Want a cuppa?'

Bella shook her head and stepped back to let him pass. 'No, you go and eat, I'll make my own tea. Anyway, I thought you were going to Sacha's café this morning with Betty and Mum?'

He took a sip of his drink and nodded. 'I am, but it's only just opened. Your mum isn't down yet either. I thought I'd wait for her to surface. She seemed tired last night, which isn't surprising when you think how far she's travelled.' He lowered his voice, 'And knowing Claire, she will have travelled as cheaply as possible.'

He was right. 'She probably took twice as long to get here too because of it.'

'I presumed the two of you were chatting into the small hours,' he said. 'So I didn't want to disturb her just yet.' He took a bite of his toast and went to sit down at the log burner which, Bella noticed, was still just about alight. 'Want me to pop in another log?'

She nodded. 'May as well. Mum is used to a much warmer climate and I don't want her to have to come downstairs to a cold room.'

She went to the worktop and put a couple of pieces of left-over cabbage loaf into the toaster, before leaning against the door frame to watch him.

'What have you got planned for today then?' Jack brushed crumbs off his sweatshirt onto the rug. 'Damn.'

'Leave it,' she said, noticing him trying to pick up the crumbs. 'Never mind me. How did last night go? You weren't back by the time Mum and I went to bed.' She hesitated briefly. 'We were a little concerned for you both.'

'It was a bit of a performance, checking his boat was secure, but we sorted it out in the end. We got chatting afterwards, which is really what delayed me.'

Irritated to have spent an almost sleepless night fretting about him, Bella said, 'You could have sent us a text or something to let us know you were both okay.'

'Yes, sorry. I only thought of that when I was nearly back at the cottage and then you were both asleep, so I crept in.'

Bella didn't like to tell him that she had been awake for hours. 'You must have been very quiet, for once.'

'I was,' he said, studying her face. 'I didn't want to wake either of you. You okay?'

'I'm perfectly fine,' she said, biting back a retort. 'Anyway, enough about that. I'll be moving things around today and will need to vacuum afterwards, so don't worry about crumbs.'

Smelling her toast burning, she rushed back to turn off the toaster and rescue it. 'I've got a market to go to. The Autumn Market at The Oaks,' she shouted. 'I'm sorting out the bits I'm taking there this morning, then taking the big things like dressers, a desk and some chairs there this afternoon,' she added, buttering her toast and pouring on runny honey bought from the previous market she'd taken part in.

She made her tea and then went to join him in the living room.

'Will they be safe leaving them there overnight?'

Bella nodded. 'The barn where my stuff will hopefully be sold is locked each evening. Tomorrow, I'll go up early with the vintage suitcases packed with my smaller goods.'

'Will you need a hand taking stuff there?'

Bella pictured Lexi's relieved reaction if she didn't have to help lift the heavier items. 'That would be brilliant,' she said, forgetting her annoyance at him.

'Shall I ask Lexi if we can borrow that estate car of hers to transport everything?' He put the final piece of crust into his mouth and chewed.

'I'm sure she won't mind, as long as her dad's not using it to deliver his paintings to clients.'

'Great. I'll go up and see her at her cottages, then I can collect it at the same time, if it's available. I'm free all day to do anything you need me to.' He stood and walked through to the kitchen. 'The only plan I have is treating your mum and Betty to breakfast, but after that I'm all yours, if you want me?'

She knew what she would have liked to answer but resisted. 'That would be great, thanks, Jack.'

'I'll go and check on Betty,' he said, 'but I'll be back soon.'

After finishing her breakfast, Bella heard her mother humming in the shower. She checked her watch, relieved. She didn't want Betty, who she knew to be an early riser, to have to wait too long for her breakfast.

She washed up her plate and cup just as footsteps came down the wooden staircase.

'Morning, Mum,' she called, wiping up her plate at the bottom of the stairs. 'Sleep well?'

'Wonderfully,' Claire said, smiling. 'Is Jack back?'

'He is. He's gone to Betty's, but he'll be back in no time. I'll quickly jump in the shower.'

Ten minutes later, Bella joined Claire in the living room. She was pleased to note that her mother did look more refreshed than she had the previous evening. 'You ready to go?'

'I am,' Claire said, pulling on a brightly coloured knitted jacket. 'I've been looking forward to this. I can't remember the last time I ate a proper English breakfast. It's going to be a treat.'

'It is,' Bella said, wishing now that she had accepted Jack's invitation to join them.

'You're not coming with us?'

'No.' Bella placed her plate in the rack above the sink. 'I'm sorely tempted to but have a market tomorrow and really need to get on and sort out what bits I'm taking.'

Jack opened the front door and beamed at Claire. 'Good morning, lovely lady,' he said. 'Ready for the off?'

'I am,' she said, stopping to kiss Bella on the cheek before joining Jack at the front door. 'Let's go. I'm famished.'

'Me, too,' Jack said, linking arms with her. 'Last chance to change your mind and join us,' he grinned, tempting Bella in more ways than one.

'No, thanks. I'll see you both later. Enjoy.'

He closed the door behind them. Bella listened to her mother's giggles as Jack chatted to her. She was grateful to him for giving her mother something fun to do on her first day at the boardwalk. She felt guilty that she would be working today and tomorrow and not giving her mother her undivided attention. But times were hard, and she didn't seem to get booked for her hand modelling work as often as she used to. The markets brought in some income, as did her tiny antique business and having lodgers, but she needed to keep on top of it and carefully watch every penny she spent.

She didn't have time to think about it now, though. She had a market stall to prepare for and needed to choose which items Jack could help her take to The Oaks.

Bella set to work, marking each item with a price that she knew most market goers would hope she'd bring down. She knew from experience that buyers enjoyed seeing larger items and settled on an art deco walnut dressing table. She had fallen in love with the item after seeing it at an elderly friend of her nan's who'd had to move into a home and sell most of her precious furniture.

Bella thought of her meeting with the old lady and how she had had to hold back her emotions when pricing up the items in her house in town.

'I've lived here all my married life,' she had said with less emotion than Bella, it seemed. 'I don't mind down-sizing, but this is the only part that I find difficult. My Brian bought me most of these bits for anniversaries and the like. But this is my favourite piece.'

She had waved Bella through to her bedroom where, against the furthest wall, was a fine piece that, although to some might look like a small occasional table with its fine straight legs and unadorned wood, Bella knew from a similar piece she had seen years ago in an auction, was a dressing table.

'Open it,' the old lady had said, proud and excited to be able to show it to someone new.

Bella had put down her notepad and pen and walked over to stand in front of it. She'd carefully lifted the top to reveal a mirror attached underneath. Then, sliding the mirrors aside she had gasped as a neat array of crystal boxes and bottles, each with a solid silver lid monogrammed with a G, were revealed.

'That's for my name, Grace,' the old lady had told Bella, her eyes shining suspiciously, as if she was about to cry.

'These are magical,' Bella had whispered. 'Please can I lift one out and look at it?'

'Help yourself, my dear.'

She'd chosen a flat round container and, after lifting it from its designated area in the dressing table, took off the lid and smiled. 'It still has the powderpuff inside, and face powder.'

Grace had nodded. 'It does. I always used it when I was going to a dance or anywhere special and wanted to be made up to look my best,' she'd said, thoughtfully. 'Those were the days. We used to go out to dinner dances and parties every week back then.' She'd stared at the glass box in Bella's hand. 'I miss those days, if I'm honest.'

'I can always take you out,' Bella had said, replacing the container carefully into its crafted holder. 'I can't promise you dancing, but we can always go out for dinner.'

Grace had raised her left hand and held it against Bella's cheek. 'You're a good girl, you are. Your nan always said you were the sweetest girl, and she was right.'

Since then, Bella had taken Grace out only once, and she'd then moved into the home and met new friends and insisted that she was happiest staying in with them.

Bella suspected that Grace was trying to be kind and not be a burden and so had tried on several occasions to persuade her to accompany her out, but the answer had always been a kind no.

Bella took a deep breath and decided that as much as she

hated parting with the dressing table, it was rather magnificent and should sell quickly. It would have to be taken to the market. Next, she looked at a matching wardrobe that Grace had also sold her, wishing she could keep them both for a time in the future when she could afford to replace her own bedroom furniture with items as luxurious as these. Now, though, especially as she didn't have Alessandro's rent coming in, she needed hard cash. Her eye was drawn by the headboard and two matching walnut bedside cabinets.

'Damn,' she said, stroking the dressing table and wishing she didn't have to try and sell it. 'Never mind, they are only things, and if Grace has the balls to part with them, then I really haven't got any reason not to.'

Thinking of Grace and her determination to rid herself of all that she couldn't take with her, Bella braced herself and pressed on.

An hour later her mother and Jack came back from the café. She heard them giggling outside the front door before either of them entered.

'Tasty breakfast?' Bella asked, sitting back on her haunches from where she had been rummaging around in a wooden linen chest.

'The best,' her mum said, coming over to see what she was doing. 'What's in there?'

'Nothing exciting,' Bella said, lifting out some fabrics that had been in the chest since it arrived. 'The owner never emptied it and I haven't had a moment to before now.'

'Well, let's have a look at them, then.' Claire reached down to pull out a piece of striped fabric. Holding it up to inspect it, she frowned. 'This isn't very exciting. I wonder why anyone thought to keep it?'

'No idea,' Bella said. 'I can't even remember who I bought it from. It's been at the back of this lot for a couple of years. No one has ever shown any interest in it, but I think the chest is James I, so it's very old.'

'The wood is too heavy and dark,' Claire said. 'I suppose everyone wants lighter furniture now. This is very unfashionable.'

'I know,' Bella agreed, sighing. 'It's such a shame. People will pay hundreds of pounds for something that will only last a few years but overlook beautifully hand-crafted pieces like this one. They're useful, too.'

Jack came over to see what they were talking about. 'I see what you mean,' he said. 'If you can't sell it, why don't you keep it and put it to some use?'

She would love to, but there wasn't any spare room in this tiny cottage. Bella told him and added, 'I can't believe I haven't cleared it out before now. I just forgot all this was inside the chest.'

'Well, there's no time like right now,' Jack said. 'Pass that material over to me and let's have a proper look at it. You can then either sell it, or use it for something. Are you going to sell the chest tomorrow?'

'I'll certainly try,' Bella said, lifting a few samples of the material out and handing them to him. 'There's more,' she said, peering inside, surprised. 'And more.'

Claire began looking through the material. 'Hey, some of this is from the fifties and sixties,' she said, excitement in her voice. 'I'm sure you'll find lots of people who want to buy it. Everyone seems keen on upcycling furniture now, and re-covering chairs and the like.'

She was right. Bella's spirits soared when she'd finished unloading the chest and inspected the materials her mother was indicating. Each sample was covered in different patterns, each with blues and yellows, greens and yellows, and reds and blacks.

'They are spectacular,' she said, delighted. 'You're right, these will be very popular. I'll have to check up on the correct asking price for them,' she added, thoughtfully. 'I don't want to over or under charge people.'

'What will they do with them?' Jack asked, studying one with a confused frown on his face. 'I can't see that this material is strong enough to be used for seating on chairs.'

Claire laughed. 'Not everyone is as heavy as you. I've seen the way you land on chairs rather than take a seat.'

He pulled a face at her. 'Not all of us are dainty little creatures like you two, are they?'

Bella checked through each one. She suspected she had at least twenty-two samples and wondered what the previous owner had collected them for. 'Maybe she was a seamstress?' she suggested. 'I think though, that if I don't sell them, then maybe I could make some curtains and matching cushions. Then sell the sets at future markets.' She raised her eyebrows and looked at her mum for reassurance.

'Sounds like a good plan,' Claire agreed.

'Where do you want me to put them?' Jack asked.

'I suppose we'd better put them back in the chest for now,' Bella said, surveying her messy room. 'This place really is too small for anything to be out of place.'

'What else are you thinking of taking to the market?' Claire asked, looking from one of Bella's treasures to the next. 'There is so much to choose from here.'

'I know.' Bella put her hands on her hips and stared from a silver candlestick to bookcases and vases. 'I suppose I'll take a mixture of styles and items. Some candlesticks, vases, a couple of chairs.'

'Costume jewellery?' Claire asked, picking up a jet opera necklace from a display box next to her.

'Yes, that always sells well.' Bella spotted some velvet-framed pictures resting on the mantlepiece. 'I love those,' she said. 'I only bought them a few months ago. They're painted on copper and are a matching pair. Each telling a story. What do you think?'

'They're lovely,' Claire said. 'Though not my style, but I can see why someone would appreciate them.'

'Right, shall I grab some boxes and help you pack these things up then?' Jack asked.

'Good plan,' Bella said. 'I'll choose the items and pass them to you and Mum to pack, if that's okay.'

They spent an hour packing, and then moving furniture around so that the bedroom suite Bella had decided to take to the market was easy to manoeuvre out of the cottage and into the car later on.

Finally finished, Claire puffed out her cheeks. 'Well, that was an effort,' she said. 'I don't know how you do all this by yourself when we're not here.'

'It just takes longer, that's all.' Bella couldn't help feeling amused at their surprise that she usually did this alone. 'Sometimes Lexi or Jools come and help me, and Sacha when she's free.'

'I couldn't do this for a living,' her mum said.

'I love buying and selling antiques and this comes with the territory,' Bella said.

'How about a walk on the beach for a breather,' Jack said. 'I can go and fetch Lexi's car and help you load this lot?'

'Good idea,' Claire said. 'Better wear a coat and scarf, it's nippy out there today despite the sun.'

Coats and scarves on, Bella and Jack stepped out from the

warmth of the untidy cottage to the boardwalk waiting for her mother to join them.

Bella breathed in the salty cold air and held it in her lungs for a few seconds, relishing the soothing qualities it released inside her. 'I couldn't bear to live anywhere else, do you know that?'

'I think this will be warm enough,' Claire said, buttoning up her jacket and smiling as she stared out to sea.

'I think so.' Bella noticed she hadn't bothered to shut the front door behind her, so went and pulled the door closed, locking it. 'Mum, it might be safer here than most places,' she said. 'But we can't go out and leave our front doors open nowadays.'

'Sorry, sweetheart, I'll be sure to remember next time.' Claire bent to pick up a small piece of driftwood at the top of the granite steps before descending to the beach. 'I always dreamt about leaving, and going as far away from this place as possible,' she said, brushing sand from the wood which was rounded by its time in the sea. 'I couldn't wait to find some fun and reinvent myself.'

Bella and Jack joined her at the bottom of the stairs, and Bella caught Jack looking sad. She watched as he walked slightly ahead, hands pushed into his pockets, head down, staring at the wet sand.

Bella supposed his sadness was caused by his issues with Nicki and wondered what must have been said the evening before when they had met for a chat. She yearned to put her arms around him and give him a hug; to put a smile back on his handsome face, but knew she couldn't do it without him realising she had a bit of a crush on him. He looked up and caught her watching him and immediately smiled. Taking his hands out of his pockets, he reached down to pick up a piece of opaque blue glass.

'It's freezing out here. Why don't we have a quick five-minute beachcombing competition to see who can find the most pieces of glass, or pottery?'

Bella wasn't surprised when her mother immediately agreed. 'Go on then,' she said, not wishing him to see how relieved she was that he had cheered up slightly. 'Let's split up and meet back at the stairs in five minutes.' Bella checked her watch. 'Right, go!'

Bella watched Jack run for a few yards. Her heart pounded. She couldn't help imagining what it must be like to be taken in his arms and kissed. *Lucky Nicki.* Stupid Nicki, for trying to make him return with her to London.

'Stop daydreaming about Jack,' her mother whispered, snapping Bella out of her reverie. 'Get looking for glass. If he catches you gazing at him like a lovelorn teenager he's going to know you've got a thing for him.'

She turned to her mother and opened her mouth to argue.

Claire raised a finger and shook her head. 'Don't waste your time, young lady,' she smiled, giving Bella a kiss on the cheek. 'I might live away, but I know you well enough to be able to read you like a favourite romantic novel. Now...' She pretended to look at something in her hand and spoke through the side of her mouth. 'He's looking over here and probably wondering why he's the only one taking part in this mini competition.' She pushed Bella lightly. 'Go and scavenge, before he suspects what's going on.'

Bella didn't need telling twice. She should have known her mother would have worked out how she felt about Jack. Claire had always been perceptive, especially when you didn't want her to be. Bella spotted a small shiny orb in the wet sand and bent down to inspect it. Picking it up carefully between two fingers, she wiped it against her trouser leg and saw that it was a marble, but a very old one. She popped it into her jacket pocket and carried on walking slowly along the beach, by the tidemark where the sea had most recently reached its height at high tide.

She could hear Jack cheering and it made her smile. She glanced over and saw him wiping a small piece of something in his hand before dropping it in his trouser pocket. She heard a seagull calling out for its mate and watched as two of them swooped and dived near to the café. Someone must have brought food outside, she decided, looking to see if it was anyone she knew.

'Hey, Dilly Daydream,' Jack called. 'Are you still with us, or are you more interested in those birds?'

'Shut up, Jack,' she said, unable to help laughing at his teasing. 'I'm doing fine, thank you very much. I'm looking forward to seeing what treasures you've discovered.' She pulled up her sleeve and checked her watch. 'Only two minutes left.' She really didn't have a clue when the five minutes were up, but thought it would give her enough time to find a few more bits to add to her marble.

Spotting a strange-shaped pebble, Bella bent to pick it up and brushed off the excess sand. There was nothing beautiful about it, but she liked its shape and in the absence of any gems, this would have to do.

'Okay, time up,' Claire called, coming back to join them. 'Hold out your hands and let's see what we've all found.'

Jack liked Bella's marble. 'I haven't seen anything like that before,' he said, examining the odd-shaped stone. 'What do you think of this?'

She picked up the opaque ruby-coloured bottle stopper, its shine dimmed by years of being washed against grains of sand, and smiled. 'You can still clearly see what it was originally,' she said, studying it from all angles. 'Which is amazing, bearing in mind that it's been bashed about in the sea for years. I love it,' she admitted. She placed it back in Jack's palm and turned to Claire. 'Mum? What did you find?'

Her mother gave her a telling look, so that Bella couldn't miss the surreptitious message that her main discovery had been about Bella's secret feelings towards Jack. She glared at her mother. 'Well? Are you going to show us, or not? I've got to go back to the cottage and start packing the heavy stuff, I can't hang around here much longer.'

Claire smiled. 'Here.' She opened her hand to reveal a heart-shaped stone made from a worn-down brick.

'It's beautiful,' Bella said, examining it. 'What do you think, Jack? Who's the winner?'

He looked from Bella to Claire and with a twinkle in his eyes said, 'It has to be the heart, doesn't it?'

6

Bella returned to the cottage, unsure what, if anything, Jack had meant. She stopped at the open door of her cottage and watched as Jack ran off in the direction of the hill to Lexi's house. Relieved to have a moment to gather her thoughts while he fetched Lexi's car, she decided almost immediately it was simply her wishful thinking that his words had been a declaration of his feelings.

She stared at her reflection in the nouveau mirror in her hallway and pulled a face at it. 'You are an idiot.'

'I think that's a bit harsh, darling,' Claire said, entering the cottage.

Not wishing to discuss her feelings for Jack, Bella focused on pulling out packed boxes of treasures from inside larger pieces of furniture. 'Help me with this, will you, Mum?'

'You can change the subject as much as you like,' Claire said, taking the second box from inside the wardrobe and carrying it over to where Bella had placed the first one. 'But we both know that as darling a man as Jack is, and he is,' she raised her eyebrows and winked at Bella. 'He will need a bit of a nudge where you're concerned.'

Intrigued, Bella stopped what she was doing and stared at her. 'Why? What makes me so different?'

Claire placed a hand on Bella's right shoulder. 'Sweetheart, I might have lived away more than I've lived here, but even I remember him asking you out when you were teenagers and you turning him down flat.'

So did she. The memory still made her cringe. She also wished she could forget his humiliation when his friends teased him for weeks after she rebuffed him.

'Didn't he kiss you once, after that?'

Bella nodded. 'I was sixteen that time,' she said, recalling only too clearly how Sacha had gone mad. 'He's Sacha's big brother,' she said, wondering how many times she wished her best friend hadn't made her promise never to go out with him. 'And anyway, he shouldn't have asked me out in front of all our friends at that earlier beach party.'

'Poor lad, your nan was mortified for him.'

'I know,' Bella said, wincing. 'She gave me a right telling off. I didn't intentionally humiliate him though. It was just how it happened.'

'That's as maybe,' Claire said. 'But despite that being years ago, maybe he still assumes you're not interested in him.'

'I think you could be right,' she said, sighing miserably, wondering how it would have been between them if things were different.

Jack was always the best looking and fittest boy in their group and she would have given almost anything to be his girlfriend. Anything, but her friendship with Sacha, and nothing was going to change the fact that Sacha was Jack's sister and that she had made a solemn promise to her never to date him.

'Surely Sacha would think differently now?'

'Maybe, but she made such a fuss, for months, until I stopped mentioning it. I daren't broach the subject now. I think she assumes we're just really close friends, which we are.' Bella paused. 'Anyway, I'm not sure he is actually interested in me. That could stir up a whole new problem. I love him living here, and don't want to mess it up.'

Claire thought for a moment. 'You could always pull on your big girl pants and ask him?'

'Ask who?' Jack said, pushing the door open. Bella glared at her mother. Why did she never think to close doors properly? 'And why are you talking about pants?'

Horrified that he'd walked in on them, and hoping he hadn't heard anything more of their conversation, Bella shook her head, trying not to show how flustered she felt. 'Just Mum talking nonsense. Thanks for collecting the car, Jack,' she said. 'Can we start loading those larger items first, then these smaller boxes can go on top.'

'No problem.' He and Claire helped her load the bigger items of furniture.

'I think that's as much as we can fit in,' he said twenty minutes later, studying the small spaces. 'Though a couple of boxes can be left at the market overnight.'

Bella showed him the rest of the things she wanted to take.

'Why don't you put some boxes inside the wardrobe and bedside cabinets,' Claire suggested with a wide, satisfied smile on her face.

'Clever lady,' Jack said, motioning for Bella to follow him back into The Bee Hive to collect them. 'These should be safe overnight if you lock them in with the furniture, shouldn't they?'

Bella agreed, relieved that she would have fewer things to take to the market early the following morning.

She got into the passenger seat of the car and waited for Jack to hand her two more boxes, putting one in the footwell between her knees and the other on her lap. 'This is getting rather claustrophobic,' she said when her mother stopped Jack to chat to him about what they were all going to do for lunch. 'Mum,' she interrupted, 'why don't you go back to the café and Sacha will give you lunch. Tell her it's on me and I'll settle up with her when I finish unloading this lot.'

Her mother stuck out her tongue at Bella and gave her a wink. 'You'd better get a move on,' she said to Jack. 'Otherwise my bossy daughter will have one of her tempers.'

They got into the car and put on their seat belts. Jack glanced at Bella as he started the ignition, before reversing the car slowly along the boardwalk.

'What my mother just said.' She cleared her throat, irritated with Claire for joking and making Jack doubt her. 'She's only referring to my tempers when I was little. My nan always teased me, saying that my terrible twos were more like the foul fours because they went on for so long. I'm not like that now.'

She wished she could shut up and stop explaining herself to him. Jack had known her long enough to be aware that most of the time she was level-headed and certainly not prone to tantrums. She did have a temper, but only when pushed to the limit.

'Take no notice,' Jack said. 'My dad is always teasing me about things that I did when I was a tot. Damn.'

'What's the matter?'

'If I'd had any sense I'd have reversed this thing to your cottage when it was still empty.'

'Good point,' she said, sitting back in her seat so he had a clear vision of the car's wing mirrors. 'I never thought of that.'

Finally, they reached the end of the boardwalk. 'I won't make that mistake again,' he said, turning the car around. 'It wouldn't be so bad if this was my car, or if I was used to driving it.' He tilted his head at Bella. 'And, as for your tantrums, I can only remember one and that was a full out fury.'

'When?' she asked, unable to recall the incident.

'You know,' he said, smiling. 'That time you caught some bloke nicking from your nan's place. It was during the summer, about ten or so years ago?'

She thought back. Recalling the lanky, greasy-haired man grabbing one of her nan's silver candlesticks from a table near her doorway and making a run for it, her irritation with him returned. 'I remember chasing him down the boardwalk,' she said. 'But I couldn't catch up with him.' She smiled at Jack, remembering he had come to her aid. 'You were coming off the beach after a surf. You chased after him.'

'Yes,' Jack laughed. 'Best unintentional rugby tackle I ever did. Bruised my right knee for weeks, that did.'

'Gave that idiot a fright though. Never saw him down here again.'

'Your nan was most impressed and bought me a big breakfast at the café.'

Bella giggled. 'Which Sacha refused to take payment for.'

They sat in companionable silence for a few moments. Their eyes locked and Bella wished she could have more of these moments alone with Jack.

'That's why I love it here so much,' he said eventually. 'It's the close-knit community. We all look out for one another, but at the same time respect each other's privacy.'

Bella thought of his aunt, Rosie, and smiled. 'Maybe Aunt Rosie can be a little bit nosy at times,' she joked.

He nodded. 'Yes, but only when it's something titillating. She's not interested in the mundane.'

His mobile rang but instead of checking to see who it was, Jack shrugged. 'It'll be Nicki wanting to have another go at me.'

He lowered his voice. 'I've given Nicki her own ringtone, so I know when it's her calling.'

'Clever move,' Bella said, liking the idea.

They drove for a few minutes along the narrow country lanes, stopping to let cars pass in the opposite direction, or slowing down to pass horses and riders on their way for a gallop on the beach.

She spotted the familiar sign, jutting into the road from a granite gatepost and pointed. 'The market is in there.'

Jack indicated and turned slowly in through the gateway and down the long gravel drive. 'Ah, yes. I know this place. Shall I park behind the house?' he asked as they both gazed in admiration at the recently renovated farmhouse.

'Yes, at the back by the courtyard of outbuildings. We need to park near the large barn. My stock will go in there overnight.'

'This is some place they've got here now they've finished working on it,' he said, giving a whistle between his teeth. 'Could you leave the boardwalk to live somewhere like this?'

'No,' she said, without hesitation.

Jack helped her unpack the car and set up at the area where her stall would be. 'Are you still going with Lexi, Sacha and Jools to the black butter-making event tonight?' he asked, referring to a Jersey speciality, which wasn't actually butter, but a spiced apple conserve.

Bella winced. She had completely forgotten about the annual event which she usually attended with her three closest friends. It had become one of their traditions. Betty always accompanied them and loved to sit with the other locals, peeling apples from local harvests for the first stage.

Jack gazed at her suspiciously. 'You'd forgotten, hadn't you?'

She nodded. 'Don't tell them, will you? I've been so busy with sorting out my stock, going to London and Mum's unexpected arrival, that it slipped my mind. Bugger.'

'You don't have to go,' he said, giving her an amused smile that told her he knew she would never back out and let the others down. He was right.

'I do. It's the last night,' she said, thinking of the laughs everyone had as they sat on their chairs, peeling thousands of apples before they were taken to be slowly cooked in a mixture of lemon juice and liquorice on an open fire in a large cauldron.

'You all seem to enjoy it.'

She smiled at the memory of last year's event. 'We do have fun,' she said dreamily. 'I love listening to the chap who plays his accordion and catching up with friends I don't see for most of the year. And that familiar smell as the butter is slowly stirred while it cooks for hours and hours. No,' she said, determined. 'I will go. But I'll need to get a move on and sort this lot out.'

Spotting an elderly couple looking a bit lost, Jack pointed at them. 'I'll just go and see if I can help over there.'

Bella watched him go. He was so unaware of the effect he had on women, especially her, with his easy ways and broad shoulders. She reminded herself that he was also kind and thoughtful, as she continued sorting through her boxes.

7

'You not ready yet?' Jack asked, entering the cottage and giving Bella a fright.

She glared at him. 'Why are you always so energetic?' she asked as he leant against the wall, the keys to Lexi's car dangling from one of his fingers. She could see he was trying to remind her of something, but what?

'The black butter making,' he said. When she kept staring at him vacantly, he added, 'I'm giving you four girls a lift there, so you can have a cider, or two.'

What was he on about? She went to stand, realising her legs were almost numb from kneeling on the floor for so long, sorting out her stock. Then it dawned on her. 'It's tonight, I forgot.'

'Again.' He laughed, shaking his head. He held out his hand and Bella gratefully took hold of it, letting him pull her up to her feet.

'How much time do I have to get ready?'

He tilted his head and glanced at his watch. 'I'd say about three minutes.'

'What?' She winced as she made her way to the stairs. 'Give me five and I'll be ready.'

Who was she kidding? she thought, hurrying up to her bedroom to change out of her creased top. The jeans would have to do. She hadn't got around to putting on a wash for a few days and was running out of suitable clothes to wear for the evening. She changed her top and washed her hands before brushing her hair and applying a little lip gloss.

Running back down to join him, she grabbed her jacket and bag and raced out of the front door, leaving Jack shaking his head in amusement.

'Come on, Jack,' she teased. 'The others will be waiting.'

She got into the car to find Sacha and Jools already sitting in the back, waiting for them. 'You're hopeless at time keeping,' Jools said.

'It's because she becomes so absorbed in what she's doing,' Sacha added. 'I suppose we all do sometimes.'

'Sorry, everyone,' Bella grinned, winding her scarf around her neck and zipping up her jacket. She noticed Betty wasn't in the car. 'I thought Betty would be here. She's okay, isn't she?' she asked, aware the older lady would hate missing out on one of her annual traditions.

'Don't worry,' Jack said. 'Your mum popped in to see her this morning for a chat. Betty was a little tired and so I said Claire and I would bring her here tomorrow morning briefly, so she's been.'

'That's kind of you,' Bella said, embarrassed not to have asked her mum if she wanted to go with her and the girls that evening. 'I'm glad Betty won't miss out completely.' She was also relieved her mum would be going at some point.

Moments later they arrived at Lexi's cottage and waited as she got into the car. 'It's very good of you to be our designated driver,

Jack,' she said, ruffling his hair and getting in the back seat next to Sacha and Jools.

'It's good of you to lend out your car, yet again.'

She sighed theatrically. 'Yes, well I was thinking that, too.'

They drove through the country lanes and St Peter's Valley towards the historical farm in St Mary where the annual event took place.

'Just drop us here,' Lexi suggested.

Jack slowed to a stop inside the entrance. A man sauntered over to the car and bent to look inside. 'More helpers for the apple peeling, I hope?'

They confirmed that they were. 'Good. You park up there, mate,' he said to Jack, 'and come and join us as soon as you can. We're a bit short-handed this evening, so you'll be very welcome to help with the stirring.'

'I...' Jack began, then seeming to change his mind, added, 'No problem. You four get out and I'll park and come straight back.'

Bella followed Lexi, Jools and Sacha into the farm where mostly women were peeling countless apples. This was the second day of the event and the peeled fruit was now being stirred in a smoky room nearby with an open fire, and a large copper cauldron-like pot she knew to call a *bachin* suspended above it. Several men, some of whom she recognised, were chatting and taking it in turns to stir the contents with a long wooden handled utensil Nan had referred to as a *rabot*. Jack arrived and was immediately called in to join them.

Bella smiled, immediately content to be among people she had known all her life. The women were shown where they could sit and immediately began taking part. As Bella sat on her wooden chair, she thought back to the first time she could recall being brought to the farm by her nan to watch the black butter – or *nier beurre* as her nan had called it – being made. Everyone had known her nan and the sense of community and love for what they were creating always gave Bella's spirits a boost.

'Can you come and help hand out some tea and cake, ma love?' one of her nan's older friends asked.

As the afternoon merged into early evening, volunteers were offered a glass of Jersey cider. Bella was grateful to Jack for driving so that the rest of them could enjoy the delicious drink, but couldn't help feeling a little sorry for him. A bellow of deep laughter filled the room, making her smile. Hearing Jack's voice, joking with the others as they kept the stirring going, reminded her that he seemed to fit in wherever he was. It made her wonder how he'd ended up with someone like Nicki, who was nothing like the people who lived in their village. Maybe it was the fact that she was so different to anyone he knew, or simply that she was the type of woman he was attracted to.

A man with an accordion arrived and began playing songs she vaguely knew from her childhood. She sang along with everyone else, noticing Jack standing at the doorway, singing along too. As the evening wore on, more apples were peeled, and as some volunteers had to leave to return home to their families, others arrived to take their place.

Pots of bean crock were brought out. Bella and Jack stood together with Jools, eating bowls full of the wholesome traditional winter food they had all been used to eating, growing up.

'I'm glad Sacha serves this at the café in the winter now,' Jack said. 'She wasn't sure how well it would go down initially, but people love it, especially the older locals and those who used to live on the island.'

Jack took their bowls from them when they had finished. Stretching before sitting down to carry on peeling apples, Bella wished she had the time to stay for the entire night. She usually liked to return for the final day, to witness the cooked spices, liquorice and lemons being added to the mixture. Nan's favourite part, she remembered, was helping put the spread into jars for selling.

She would need to be sure to buy some when it was ready. Bella never failed to have a jar in her kitchen cupboard and loved it spread on toast with a little cheese. It reminded her of winters growing up, and the Christmassy smell from the mixture made her wish that she could share this with Nan, just one more time.

She yawned.

'You're looking tired,' Jack whispered, his deep voice making her smile and cheering her up. 'It's after one and I think that maybe you four should be thinking about getting home.'

He was right. They had a busy day ahead and now that she'd stopped, she noticed how tired her neck and shoulders were from looking down for hours as she peeled the apples. 'Good point,' she said. 'I'll pass this on to someone else and wash my hands. I won't be long.'

As the women waited for Jack by the front door, Sacha grinned. 'I can hear him chatting to someone again,' she said. 'My brother has to be the most sociable person I know.'

Bella rubbed the back of her neck, relieved to hear Jack chatting as he came to join them. 'You're going to be back here again in a few hours,' she teased. 'You can talk to everyone then. Now, come along before we all pass out where we're standing.'

8

The sound of children screeching with excitement woke Bella from a deep sleep. She stretched slowly and sighed. Her back still ached from the night before.

She had enjoyed a couple of glasses of cider, too, and smiled at the thought of how Betty had been the last one ready to go home the previous year. The older lady never failed to be amused by Bella and her friends yawning and needing to get home to their beds hours before she wanted to leave.

Bella raked her hands through her bed-hair and rubbed her eyes as a nagging thought seeped slowly in to her consciousness. She tried to recall if she had forgotten something and turned to look at her alarm clock.

'Seven forty-five,' she murmured, closing her eyes, relieved that she still had half an hour before having to get up, shower and open the shop. She was grateful to the noisy children outside because she had forgotten to set her alarm. The same nagging doubt disturbed her. She sat up, pushing her fingers through her tangled hair once more. She mentally ticked off all that she needed to do for today, then looked at the clock again. What the hell was she missing?

She got up, pushed her feet into her fluffy slippers and pulled on her dressing gown. She would go and make a quick cup of tea. Reaching the bottom of the stairs she saw Claire, sitting by the fire, reading a book.

'You're up then?' Claire said, stating the obvious. 'I was going to bring you a cup of tea once I'd finished this chapter.'

'No need,' Bella said. 'Do you want a fresh one?'

'Thank you.' Claire placed one of Bella's business cards into the book and closed it. 'What time do you need to be at the market?'

'Oh no, the market! I forgot it was today.' Bella's mouth fell open in horror. She stared at her boxes, relieved that she'd at least finished packing the night before. 'I'm going to be so late.'

Her mum got up and pushed a stray strand of hair off Bella's face. 'Calm down. Go and shower, I'll wake Jack and get him to run up to Lexi's and fetch her car. You should be ready by the time he gets back. We can all load everything up. Don't panic. Now, go.'

Relieved that her mother had sprung into action, Bella did as she was told and ran up the stairs to the bathroom.

With no time to wait for the water to heat up, she leapt under the shower, gasping as the cold water hit her skin and once she'd finished, wrapped a towel around herself and prepared to rush to her room. The towel dropped, just as Jack came out of his room. She wasn't sure which of them was more shocked and gripped the towel over her front to protect her modesty, aware he could probably see her bottom as she ran down the corridor.

'Bloody hell,' she shrieked, mortified. Could this day get any more disastrous?

'I'm not looking,' he shouted.

She glanced over her shoulder to see he had covered his eyes with his hands. The vision almost made her smile.

'Your mum has phoned Lexi. I'm off to get the car,' he said, not looking at her. 'I'll be back in a few minutes.'

'Thanks!' she shouted as she closed her bedroom door. The heat in her face warmed her up, which was something. With no time to think, she quickly dressed in a T-shirt and jeans, almost falling sideways onto the bed when her foot caught on the hem. Grabbing a jumper and pulling it on, she pushed a sockless foot into a trainer, finally locating the other under the bed before running downstairs to help her mother.

'I'm back,' Jack shouted, moments later.

'Thank you so much,' she said, pointing to the heap of boxes when he raised his hands in question.

'Don't worry about what order to put them in, just let's get them in the car and up to the farm. I hope the farmer bends his rule about timing, just this once.'

She picked up a box, loaded it onto another and hurried out to the car. Claire was pushing in the first two boxes and Bella was relieved her mother wasn't the type to worry about breaking a nail and just got on with whatever needed doing.

'Thanks, Mum,' she said panting from panic. 'Just shove them in as far as possible, please.' She practically threw the boxes she was carrying into the back of the car before running back to fetch more.

She reached the door and had to jump sideways to avoid crashing into Jack, who was laden with boxes. 'You're a superstar,' she said, running inside.

Finally, the car was loaded in record time. She waved to her mother, who looked extremely relieved to see the back of them, and Jack sped the car up as soon as they'd left the boardwalk and reached the hill.

'There's a speed limit here, you know,' she said, watching out for anyone who might not see them coming.

'I'm doing fifteen, so we're still going pretty slowly,' he said, shaking his head and smiling at her. 'Relax, you'll be fine.'

'But the farmer's very strict about market rules.'

'Well, we're not there yet.' Jack stopped at a yellow line, waiting for a tractor pulling a small boat to pass them before putting his foot down on the accelerator and racing up the road. 'You leave him to me,' he said winking at her. 'I've known him since school and he's a good bloke. Once we've explained that you overslept after last night's black butter making session, I'm sure he'll take pity on you.'

She took a deep breath to calm down a little and sighed. 'I hope you're right. I don't fancy taking this lot home again, and having to do the same with the bedroom suite we took up last night.'

'It'll be fine, you mark my words,' Jack said, reducing his speed and indicating to turn into the farm driveway.

The farmer wasn't as easy to convince as Jack had expected. Bella watched Jack first trying to charm the angry looking man and then being a little sterner, finally lowering his voice and saying something to him that Bella couldn't make out. He pointed over in her direction. She smiled at him, willing him to soften.

'Fine, but just this once,' he said loudly, shaking his head. 'Hurry up and unload and park the car in the field with the other vehicles. People have started to arrive and I don't need the market to look as if we don't know what we're doing.'

'Thanks,' Bella shouted. 'I really appreciate this.'

His face relaxed and he smiled. He was probably tired from keeping the farm going, she reasoned. The market was his latest venture and it was becoming more and more popular and probably harder to keep organised.

'Why are you gawping at each other?' Jack whispered. 'I thought he wanted us to get a move on and unload the car.'

'I was returning his smile,' she said. 'Being nice.'

Jack grinned. 'Right. We should get on with this lot now though, if you've finished?'

She nudged him in his ribs.

'Ouch,' he laughed, wincing. 'What was that for?'

'Being mean.'

The stock unloaded, Bella thanked Jack and began arranging her antiques to create a presentable display.

'Damn,' she said, touching her stomach. 'I forgot to bring my bum bag.'

Jack raised his eyebrows. 'Your what?'

Amused at the shocked expression on his still-tanned face, Bella giggled. 'My bum bag. It's like a belt with a small bag attached that I keep my float in. I've stupidly left it at home. I don't have any money on me for change.'

Jack pushed his hands into each of his pockets and handed her a small amount of change with a few notes. 'Here, take this,' he said, without bothering to count it. 'It's all I have but it might tide you over for a bit. I'll go and get your... bum bag?'

'Thanks, Jack,' she said, wondering how many times she would end up having to thank him by the end of the day. 'It's hanging from the handle on my wardrobe.'

'Right, I won't be long.'

She watched him running out of the barn and her heart swelled with love for the untidy, wild-haired man who drove her best friend nuts. People often found it hard to believe that Sacha and Jack were siblings. They were very different, although both tall and blonde. Sacha was more focused on business and had to work hard not to take things too seriously, while Jack seemed to think he had all the time in the world to do whatever he felt like doing. She loved that side of him and wished she could be a little more carefree at times.

'Miss? Miss, I say, are you going to serve me or not?'

Bella snapped out of her daydream about Jack and stared wide-eyed at the little lady in front of her. The steel grey eyes narrowed in irritation as she waited for Bella to answer. 'Well?'

'I'm so sorry,' Bella apologised. 'It's been a bit of a hectic morning, with one thing and another.'

'Yes, well, I have to get back to a sick husband, so if you don't mind can we cut the chit-chat and get on?'

Bella cleared her throat. 'Yes, of course. Is there something in particular you're interested in?' She spotted the wrinkled hands were holding a string of opera pearls. 'They're lovely. Are they for you?'

The woman looked at her as if she was insane. 'No. It's my granddaughter's thirtieth and I'm looking for something special to give her for a gift. These look real, are they?'

'They are,' Bella said proudly. She would love to have kept the pearls and it had been a difficult decision to sell them, but where would she ever wear them? She pointed to the price tag. 'I think the price is reasonable.'

'How much can you take off?'

Bella was more interested in getting a sale than arguing. There wasn't much call for a set of opera pearls, she reasoned, so calculated the amount in her head that would afford her a little profit, but keep the buyer interested. 'I'll give you eleven pounds off,' she said. 'How about that?'

'Fifteen?'

'Twelve.'

'Fourteen.'

This frail little lady was tougher than she looked, which Bella knew from experience, happened often. 'Thirteen, but that's my final offer.'

The scowl from the lady's face vanished and she gave Bella the friendliest smile. 'Spectacular, thank you.' She rummaged in her bag while Bella put the pearls in a little black box with The Bee Hive printed on top in gold. The smell of cooked bacon wafted in through the barn's open doors, making Bella's mouth water. She could have kicked herself for getting up so late and not having time to eat anything before leaving the cottage.

'Here you go,' the lady said, taking out a wad of notes and counting off the right amount for Bella. They exchanged the pearls for the money and the lady nodded. 'It was good doing business with you, young lady,' she said, before looking down at the name on the box. 'The Bee Hive. I'll have to come and visit your shop sometime. There are a few things I've spotted here, but I don't have time to buy them now.' She dropped the box into her bag and took out a set of car keys. 'Where are you based?'

'On the boardwalk,' Bella said, intrigued by this woman, hoping she really would come and visit her. 'It's the blue cottage at the end.'

'Good. I might see you soon then.'

'I hope so,' Bella said, about to say something else, when a couple stopped in front of her stall. They asked about the bedroom suite but walked away after a few minutes of trying to haggle the price down far more than Bella was happy with.

'Sorry it took so long.' Jack arrived as the couple walked away from the stall. 'Is this it?' He held up her bum bag.

'Yes. Thanks so much.' She quickly secured the belt around her waist.

'Do you need any help?'

Bella liked the idea of having someone to chat to if the day passed slowly. 'That would be great.'

'You must be starving,' Jack said, after a few moments. 'There's a barbeque outside the barn, do you want me to get you a sausage or bacon roll, or something?'

She closed her eyes for a second. 'I've been tormented by the smell coming from that barbeque since it started up. Yes, please. Bring me whatever you're having.'

'Tea, or hot chocolate?' Jack asked. 'There's a yurt selling various drinks.'

'Hot chocolate, please,' she said, her mouth watering in anticipation of the treats he would soon be bringing her.

By the time Jack returned, carrying their delicious late breakfast, she had served two more people.

'It's going well so far,' she said, taking the drinks from him and placing them at the back of her table. 'This lot smells heavenly.' She breathed in the bacon roll he handed to her. 'You have been a complete superstar today.'

He took a bite from his roll and shrugged. After chewing and swallowing his mouthful, he said. 'It's my pleasure. I didn't have anything else planned anyway.'

'What about Nicki?' Bella asked, wishing she didn't feel she had to. 'Won't she be hoping to catch up with you today?'

'Never mind that,' he said, taking a careful sip of his coffee. 'Catch, would be the correct term. She's a determined woman, that one.' A shadow came over his face and he continued eating his food in silence.

Bella had seen them together once or twice. Picturing Nicki in her pristine clothes and high heels, and her immaculate shiny bob, it was hard to place her with someone like Jack. He was the typical surfer boy, with sun-bleached, long hair and too much of a free spirit to be kept in order by someone who clock-watched.

Sacha had never taken to her brother's latest girlfriend and during the summer had confided in Bella about Nicki, and why she was concerned that Jack should stick to his decision to break away from her. Bella didn't feel she was in a position to say much at all. She had her own feelings for him and couldn't go behind another woman's back and make snide comments about her to her boyfriend. How could she ever hope to be with Jack if she'd been the one to help him split from his girlfriend? Nicki might not be her friend, but there was a girl code, and Bella had no intention of breaking that, however much she might be attracted to Jack.

She finished her food and wiped her mouth with the napkin that Jack handed to her. 'Do you mind waiting here if I go and wash my hands quickly?'

'No, you go,' he said. 'You'd better leave me your strange bag though, just in case someone comes to buy something.'

She undid the clasp and handed it to him. He held up his roll and coffee for her to fasten it around his waist. Bella cleared her throat. Standing behind him, she reached around him to pass one end to her other hand. She had to press up against him, but Jack stood still, seemingly unaware that her actions were doing things to her that she could never admit to anyone. She pressed the two ends of the clips together against his hard stomach, focusing on getting it right so that she could step away as soon as possible and leave him to it before he noticed how red her face had gone.

'Won't be long,' she shouted over her shoulder without looking at him. She hurried out of the barn and crossed the courtyard to the back of the building where the toilets had been installed earlier in the year. Bella washed her hands, and as she dried them with sheets of paper towels, she stared at her reflection in the mirror above the sink. Wetting the paper, she wrung it out carefully and held it against her face, hoping the coolness of the water would reduce the redness in her face.

'You okay, love?' a lady asked.

Mortified to have been discovered acting weirdly, Bella lowered the paper and smiled. 'Fine thanks, just a little hot from unpacking my stock.'

The lady didn't look convinced, but smiled and went into one of the cubicles.

About to return to her stall, Bella was distracted by the myriad of sellers inside the courtyard. She stopped and stared from one stall to another, marvelling at all the crafts and produce. It made her proud to be local. She was sure Jack wouldn't mind if she took a few minutes to mooch around each of them.

First was the pumpkin stall, with at least thirty intricately carved pumpkins dotted on and around the table. Scary faces, and faces with fangs and autumn scenes. She made a mental note to come back and buy one of them and hoped that the medium sized pumpkin with a large bat carved into it was still waiting for her later.

She then walked over to the next stall and breathed in the smell of freshly baked loaves.

'I have to come back with some money,' she told a man in a flour-dotted apron. 'But could you tell me what you've got here?'

Another two customers came over and waited for him to explain about each of the loaves.

'This one is honey and chocolate,' he said, pointing to a darker loaf. 'The honey is local, but the chocolate isn't.' He indicated the next batch of loaves. 'These are bloomers, large and small. Then we have a soda loaf, and this one here is made with sourdough.' He picked up a large cabbage loaf. 'I'm sure if you're local, you'll know what these are.'

'Cabbage loaves,' Bella said, her mouth watering at the thought of the delicious bread.

The couple standing next to her looked baffled. 'Cabbage? That doesn't sound very bread-like, if you don't mind me saying,' the woman grimaced.

The baker shook his head. 'It isn't cabbage flavoured but baked with a cabbage leaf on the top of the dough and also one on the bottom. The taste is subtle and gives the loaf a delicious flavour. You should try one.'

'He's right,' Bella said. 'They're delicious and my favourite loaves to eat. My friend has toasted cabbage loaf on the menu at the Summer Sundaes Beach Café on the boardwalk.'

'Where is it, dear?' the man asked.

'Turn right at the gateway and keep following the road down the hill until you get to the nearest bay. If you park in the car park there, and cross over to the boardwalk, you'll find the café to the right at the end. You can't miss it.' She noticed the baker looking unhappy, so added, 'In the meantime, I really think you should buy one of these. I will be, as soon as I've fetched some money from my friend. He's manning my antique stall in the barn.'

The woman held her hands out for the baker to pass her the loaf. 'You've persuaded me,' she said, waiting while the smiling baker put the loaf into a brown paper bag. 'Pay the man, Sydney,' she said to her husband and smiled at Bella. 'Thank you, dear. We'll look forward to having this tonight with some of the local honey we've just bought. We're staying with a friend and I'm sure she'll be happy to let us use her toaster.'

Bella decided to leave them to pay for their bread and made

her way to the next stall, which was laden with knitwear and crocheted items. The stall was colourful but surrounded by people, so she kept walking. The next stall sold salted caramel sauce. She had bought some of this a few times before and loved to drizzle it on pancakes and in hot chocolate to enhance the taste. Remembering she still had a bottle at home and no money to hand she didn't stop to buy any.

'Cider. Delicious Jersey cider,' a man called from a small van with an opening on one side. She decided to come back and buy a glass for her and Jack a little later.

She noticed the time on the small clock tower and was shocked to see she had taken so long. Running back into the barn, she mouthed an apology to Jack who was trying to talk about the art deco dressing table to a beautiful young woman Bella guessed to be in her early thirties.

'I'm so sorry I was ages,' she said, smiling at the woman. 'I had a little look around the stalls and forgot the time.'

'I'm always doing the same thing,' the woman said. 'Jack's been telling me all about this magnificent piece.' She gazed up at him through long mascaraed lashes.

'Need any help?' Bella asked, not wishing to intrude if he was flirting with the woman, but not wishing to lose a sale if he didn't know how to describe the piece.

'Yes, please,' Jack said, looking relieved. 'I know this is art deco, but that's about it, I'm afraid.'

'No problem.' Bella stepped forward and opened the top of the dressing table before showing the buyer the contents. 'It really is a work of art,' she said. 'I have to be honest, if I had the space to keep it I would, but unfortunately I don't.'

'I love it,' the woman said, stroking the wood with her manicured hand. 'How much is it?'

Jack cleared his throat. 'Excuse me interrupting, but here's your money belt. I'm just going to have a look in the courtyard. Won't be long.'

'No problem. Thanks, Jack.'

Bella saw disappointment in the woman's face, so hurriedly told her more about the dressing table. Aware that buyers enjoyed hearing the provenance of their furniture, she said, 'I bought this from a woman whose husband had gifted it to her on their wedding day. She spent many happy years using it, apparently. Taking it with her when they were sent abroad to India and Rhodesia in the fifties and sixties. He was a diplomat in the Foreign Service,' she added, hoping her recollections were correct.

'I must have it,' the woman said, seeming enthralled by Bella's tale. She dipped into her bag and pulled out her purse and credit card. 'How much did you say it was?'

Bella told her the price and agreed that she would deliver the piece the following day. She hoped Lexi wouldn't mind her borrowing the car again and was relieved to have made a decent sale. She wrote down the woman's home address and mobile number, and after selling her two pieces of costume jewellery, as well as a thirties jug, wished her well and promised to see her around lunchtime the following day.

The morning went quickly. She made several further sales, but still hadn't managed to get anyone to buy the bedroom suite, despite a lot of interest. Unsure how to gain the sale, she asked Jack for ideas.

'Some people don't like asking the price,' he said. 'Maybe put a tag on each piece and then one on the wardrobe covering the entire suite. Who knows, it might work.'

It was an excellent idea. Bella did her calculations on a piece of paper and then wrote up the different price tags and tied them onto the handles. 'I hope this works,' she said. 'I was taking a chance bringing this lot, but would love to shift them and be able to afford replacement stock for the cottage. My regulars like to find new things when they come.' She ran her hand over the polished veneer of the wardrobe. 'I think I got a little carried away when I bought it all.'

Jack studied the wardrobe for a few seconds. 'It is a little too big for your living room, well, shop,' he agreed. 'Don't worry, we've got a few hours yet. Someone might be tempted to buy the lot.'

It occurred to Bella that Jack was initially only going to drop her off and help her unpack, not stay with her for the day and help sell stock. 'Don't you have somewhere you need to be?' she said, wincing when her words came out a little differently to how she had intended.

Jack's cheerful expression vanished. 'You trying to get rid of me?'

'No,' she placed her hand on his muscular forearm. 'Sorry, I didn't mean it like that. I just don't want you to feel you have to stick it out here all day, that's all. Don't you want to go and do something else now?'

He gave a slow lazy shrug. 'Not particularly,' he said. 'If I go back to the boardwalk Nicki's bound to find me. I'd rather be here with you.'

Delighted, Bella smiled. 'Oh, that's... I don't know what to say,' she said.

'Yeah, I mean, you're not going to give me a hard time, are you.'

She grinned, 'No, of course not.'

'You're a good mate, Bella. I enjoy spending time with you. It was especially fun those evenings on the beach with Sacha, do you remember?'

Of course she did. But she didn't so much like the idea that he saw her as a good mate; not when she dreamt about being so much more to him. Shut up, she thought. You're being a complete idiot. You rejected him and he is involved, whether he likes it or not, with Nicki.

'Bella?'

'What? Oh, yes, they were fun times.'

He laughed at some memory. 'Your mum's just like you. Funny and caring. She's brilliant, isn't she?'

'She is,' Bella agreed, starting to feel more miserable. So, she was his friend and just like her mother. He really didn't see her romantically at all, did he? Obviously not. Bella sighed. She noticed him looking confused by her reaction and forced a smile. 'Right, it's time I treated us to a glass of that local cider. What do you say?'

'Perfect,' he smiled, putting his arm around her and giving her a quick hug. 'Do you want me to go and fetch it?'

'No,' she said. 'I'll go.' She walked off, relieved to be able to get away from him for a moment and gather her thoughts and emotions. She hated herself for being such an idiot. What was wrong with her? She wasn't a teenager any more and should be too old to harbour secret feelings for him. Not that her mother would agree, she reasoned. But Jack had known her forever, and apart from asking her out that time, he hadn't ever let her think he felt anything for her. And he'd never tried to kiss her, since then. The thought made her miserable.

'Blimey, you could do with a snifter of this,' the man on the cider van said, holding out a glass of the pale gold liquid to her. 'This one's on me. Don't tell anyone or I'll be fired, but I hate to see a lady in distress.'

Bella took the glass and drank some. 'Delicious, thanks. But I'm fine,' she insisted.

'You're not in the best of moods though, are yer, love?'

'I wasn't. But this has hit the spot. It's incredible. Can I buy two glasses to take back to my friend?'

'Sure. Is she the one who's annoyed you?'

'She's a he, actually, and yes, but not intentionally so I've no right to be miserable with him.'

'Fancy him, do yer?'

The comment was like a slap to her face. Stunned, she glared at him. 'No.' She paid him, waited for her change and marched back to the barn, a glass of cider in each hand.

* * *

Jack's plan worked. An elderly couple who had recently downsized to a thirties cottage were delighted to spot Bella's bedroom suite. After a little negotiation, which resulted in Bella lowering the price more than she had originally intended, they agreed terms and wrote out a cheque for her.

'I'll have to let you know about collecting them though,' the husband said, rubbing his square chin thoughtfully. 'We won't be able to take them today.'

'We can drop them off to you this evening, if you like?' Jack offered.

Bella, delighted at the thought of not having to taking them back in to the cottage again, instantly agreed. 'Yes, will six-thirty suit you?'

The man took hold of his wife's hand and beamed. 'Perfect. I'll write down our address and phone number in case you can't find it. The house is only a few minutes up the hill from here, so it shouldn't take you too long to get there.'

'That's settled then.'

By the end of the day Bella was exhausted. She noticed Jack looking rather jaded, too.

'I wouldn't want to do this too often,' he said, collecting their rubbish and taking it out to the bin in the courtyard.

She watched him walking away, staring at his broad shoulders, shown off to perfection in his faded blue jumper, his muscular physique a result of his beloved water sports. She knew she would remember today for a long time, and not just because she'd made a decent amount of money.

'Thanks for offering to drop the furniture off,' she said, packing up the leftover stock and placing it carefully into the boxes to return to the car. 'It'll make such a difference at the cottage, not having them crammed into the living room.'

'I'm hoping it'll be easier to carry them into their house than your place,' he said with a wink.

Bella didn't like to ruin his triumphant moment but had to be honest with him. 'Er, it's a bedroom suite and we'll probably have to carry it upstairs.' She watched him grimace as the realisation dawned on him.

He helped her pack up the rest of the unsold items and carried them to the car with her. Bella stopped to ask the farmer whether he would mind them dropping the smaller items back at the cottage first, before coming back for the larger pieces of furniture.

'No problem at all, Bella,' he said. 'I've got a larger van if you need me to help with anything.'

'That's a brilliant idea,' Jack said, coming up behind Bella. 'I'll drop Bella home and you can help me deliver the pieces to the couple. Thanks.'

Bella didn't dare catch Jack's eye as she returned to the barn to fetch the remainder of the boxes. She suspected he'd jumped at the farmer's offer in order to get the furniture into the customers' house. It would be easier and take less time than if Bella went with him.

'Why don't you take Lexi's car home? I can ask the farmer to drop me off,' Jack said, catching up with her.

'Good point,' she said, happy to agree.

9

Bella spotted Jack coming down the hill towards the boardwalk, just as she'd dropped off the car at Lexi's, and ran to meet him.

'You were quick.' She smiled up at him as they began walking.

'I think he was in a hurry to get rid of me and return to his farm. I offered to help with the clear up after the market, but he declined. Not sure why,' Jack said. 'I would have jumped at the chance of someone helping me, especially as he was kind enough to drop off the furniture for you.'

Bella didn't understand it either. 'Never mind, we're done for the day now.'

They walked on a little in silence. A gust of wind sent leaves falling from the trees on the side of the road. Bella and Jack stepped on the ochre, yellow and golden leaves, enjoying the crunchy sound as they walked, each lost in their own thoughts.

Bella had an inspirational thought. 'Sacha mentioned you were both concerned that there might not be enough work for you at the café every day. If you like, you could always help me. I'd be happy to pay you.'

Jack stopped walking, causing Bella to retrace her steps.

'What's the matter?'

He scowled at her. 'I helped today because I wanted to spend time with a mate, I didn't expect payment for it.'

'Fine,' she snapped, irritated with him for taking offence when none was meant. 'I won't pay you for your time today then. But you'd be doing me a favour helping me out when times are busy, like today. I wouldn't want you to do it and not pay you.'

Jack pushed his hands in his pockets. 'I'm not happy with it though.'

They continued walking. 'With what?' Bella had to step in front of him to get out of the way of an oncoming car that was going too fast.

'Paying you rent and taking your money for helping out. It doesn't seem right, that's all.'

Exasperated, Bella tried to work out the best way to get him to agree to her proposal. 'Does Sacha pay you when you work at the café?'

'Yes.'

'So? What's the difference?'

Jack sighed heavily.

She took hold of his arm and pulled him to face her. 'Tell me, what's the difference? Your sister paying you, or me paying you? I don't get it.'

He took her by the shoulders and stared at her. Lowering his head to her height, he was about to say something, when someone called out his name.

'Nicki?' Jack said, almost to himself. He dropped his hands from Bella's shoulders and stepped back as if he'd been caught doing something wrong.

Nicki shouted and waved. 'Jack, where the hell have you been all day? I've been searching for you. No-one knew where you were.'

She marched towards them and narrowed her eyes when she saw who was with him. 'Belinda, isn't it?' she asked.

Bella knew Nicki was fully aware of her name but smiled sweetly. She was sure Nicki was trying to bait her and she had no intention of giving her that satisfaction. 'Jack's been helping me.'

'You? Why?' She glared at Jack.

Bella watched the intensity of her focus on him and could see why Jack was finding it difficult to break away from someone so determined. She opened her mouth to explain, when Jack spoke first.

'Bella needed help with her antique stall at the market today. I'm just back from helping her deliver some furniture to a couple of buyers.' His voice was level but Bella could sense from his steely tone that he wasn't impressed at having to explain his whereabouts. 'What did you need me for?'

Nicki ignored Bella. Stepping in front of her, she linked her arm with Jack's. 'You know we have a lot to discuss,' she said, pulling him forward. 'Come with me to the hotel bar, I've got a proposition for you.'

Bella didn't like the sound of that. Not wishing to give Nicki the satisfaction of being interested, Bella pulled up the collar of her coat.

'You okay to get home alone?' Jack asked.

Bella smiled at him. 'Perfectly, thanks. And Jack?' she called after them a few seconds later.

'Yes?'

'Thanks again for everything today. You've been amazing. I owe you one.'

Jack gave her a half smile. Bella could see by the twinkle in his eyes that he was amused at her snipe back at Nicki.

She ambled along, letting them increase the distance between them, and wondered exactly what proposal Nicki might have for Jack. She could imagine it was something intended to try and persuade him to return to the mainland with her. She couldn't really blame Nicki. After all, wouldn't she want to keep Jack if he was her boyfriend? Of course she would.

She arrived back at the cottage to find the living room light beaming out onto the boardwalk. Her mum must be home. Bella smiled. She liked the idea of arriving home to the lights on and the fire roaring. It was so much more welcoming than arriving home to an empty cold house. Although she loved being her own boss, and living alone when there was no one renting her rooms, it could get a bit lonely sometimes. Working from home meant she was usually at the cottage when her tenants came home. If she knew them, like Jack and Alessandro, she liked to be there to welcome them back for the evening. If she didn't, then she didn't like to chance someone being a little light-fingered and taking one of her small silver spoons, or maybe an ornament or vase that could fit easily into a bag.

It had happened once before. A couple she had thought to be as trustworthy as they were friendly, stole a small oil painting from one of her stands by the front door. It couldn't have been anyone else and had upset her deeply. Since then, she had been more cynical when it came to her lodgers, which is why she was happy to have Alessandro and Jack there.

'Hi, Mum,' she called stepping into the warmly lit room and walking over to stand in front of the fire to warm up before taking off her coat and scarf.

'I'll be down in a sec,' Claire called.

Bella rubbed her hands together and stared into the flames. This was more like it, she thought. Arriving home to a warm cottage and someone to talk to about her day.

She undid her coat and taking it off, went over to hang it up on the coat hooks along the wall near the front door. She was used to keeping the place tidy so as not to have to clean up after herself each morning before opening the shop. She took off her boots and carried them upstairs to her bedroom. Bella drew her curtains. There was little point leaving them open. She might be able to hear the waves rolling and crashing on the sandy beach outside but couldn't see very much now that it was dark.

She changed out of her jeans and jumper and into jogging bottoms and an over-large grey hoodie with I Love New York on the front that she had bought several years ago during a long, spring weekend there with Sacha, Lexi and Jools. She looked across to the wooden framed photograph of the four of them, that she'd asked a passer-by to take on the seventy-fifth floor of the Rockefeller Center, with the iconic figure of the Empire State Building in the background.

It had been a memorable trip and she knew that her friends would love to take another holiday together. Picking up the photo, Bella sat on her bed. So much had changed since then. Sacha had taken over the running of the Summer Sundaes Beach Café, Jools had to look after her grandmother much more since her Parkinson's had worsened and she was confined to a wheelchair most days, while Lexi had her three fisherman's cottages to keep immaculate for the holiday season, which now seemed to last most of the year.

'One day,' she said dreamily, placing the photo of the four of them – Jools making bunny ear signs behind Lexi's head as they beamed at the camera – back on the dressing table.

Her room was a little chilly, so Bella hurriedly pushed her feet into the fluffy slippers that Jools had bought her the previous Christmas. The memory reminded her that it wouldn't be too long until Christmas came around again. She loved the idea of having Jack and Alessandro in the cottage, and wondered whether her mother would still be on the boardwalk, or if she'd have tired of island life and returned to Sri Lanka. She hoped not.

10

'You'll never guess what,' Jools said, pushing her hands through her spiky pink hair the following morning. 'Gran heard Jack's ex telling the manager of the hotel that she's planning a secret wedding for her and her fiancé.'

'She can't do that,' Bella said, horrified. 'Jack is the last person you could force into a surprise wedding.'

'That's up to him to decide though, isn't it?' Mrs Jones, Jools' grandmother, looked up from the figures she was working on at the till in the second-hand bookshop she and Jools ran together. Despite knowing the lady her entire life, Bella – and everyone else on the boardwalk – still referred to her as Mrs Jones. 'Jack's a big lad,' she said. 'I'm sure he can stand up for himself against that little madam.'

But what if he can't? Bella thought. Should she tip him off about Nicki's plans?

'And don't you go saying anything to him,' Jools' grandmother said. 'I shouldn't have been earwigging her conversation. And certainly shouldn't have told you girls.'

'Why not, Mrs Jones?' Bella asked, desperate to be able to share this information with him.

'Because, Bella, it's not your business, nor yours either, young lady,' she said, pointing at Jools.

'Then why tell us, if we can't do anything with the information?'

'Stop moaning and help me sort these books,' she said, pushing them across the counter to Jools. 'Betty had them brought in to me this morning on consignment. We need them marked up and displayed to sell them for her as quickly as possible.'

At the mention of Betty's name, concern coursed through Bella. She, like everyone else on the boardwalk, was extremely fond of the oldest and most heroic resident. Bella still felt emotional at the thought of the plaque the residents had erected to honour Betty's actions during the Occupation of the island during the Second World War.

'Does she need money, do you think?' she asked, not sure how she could help her out if she did.

'Nothing like that, Bella,' Mrs Jones said, lifting another three hardbacks out of the box next to her before checking them and passing them on to Jools. 'She's wanting to clear a little space in that cottage of hers. She's taken in a rescue cat that someone abandoned near here. She wants a place for its bed.'

Bella liked the idea of Betty having a companion living in her cottage. 'That is good news. How did she find out about it?'

'Young Jack Collins,' Mrs Jones said. 'He met up with someone when he was drying off after a surf and they got chatting. The woman told him about the cat and he presented it to Betty the next day with a bed, food and bowls. She was delighted, apparently.'

Bella couldn't imagine why he hadn't mentioned it. 'He never said.'

Jools stroked her arm. 'Maybe he forgot, or perhaps he didn't want to show off about giving her the cat. Who knows?'

Talking about Jack reminded Bella about Nicki and her plans for a secret wedding. 'I don't see how I can keep Nicki's plans to myself, Mrs Jones.'

'Well, you must. It's not our secret to tell. Promise me you won't tell him.' She gave Bella a piercing glare that she remembered only too well from when Mrs Jones was her headmistress at secondary school. 'Yes, I promise.'

'Good, now off you go. We need to get these books sorted for Betty.'

'No problem. See you soon.' As Bella left, she tried to think of a way to tell Jack without breaking Mrs Jones' confidence. 'Bugger,' she groaned. There had to be a way of helping him with this.

She returned to the cottage to find Jack sitting in his favourite forties armchair, dozing by the fire. Bella crept into the living room and watched his muscular chest rise and fall under his faded blue sweatshirt. His dark lashes, fanned out on his cheeks, were the envy of most women who knew him. Why did men seem to have all the luck when it came to long lashes? she thought. He looked so peaceful and relaxed. What would he want her to do? He was her friend and she owed it to him to be honest. Then again, as Mrs Jones insisted, it wasn't Bella's secret to share. And she had promised not to say anything.

Her guilt intensified until she remembered that he was a grown man and more than capable of standing up for himself and saying no, should he choose to. She leant against the small davenport desk near the front door. Could it simply be that she was scared he might want to say yes to Nicki's proposal? Would he? Before she could answer her own question, Jack opened his eyes and caught her staring.

'I didn't hear you come in. Been back long?' His grin disappeared. 'You look very pensive. Something wrong?'

She forced a smile. 'No, everything's fine.'

He sat up and narrowed his eyes, leaning forward. 'Why do I get the impression you're fibbing to me, Bella?' he smiled. 'You can confide in me about anything. I hope you know that?'

She stood up and waved her hand in front of her face, as if a pesky fly was flitting about in front of it. 'I was just thinking about, um modelling work.'

'You've got another job? That's great news.'

She shook her head, unable to tell him a downright lie. 'No, unfortunately not. I think Megan Knight and I got off to a bit of a rocky start. I was wondering when I'm going to be offered another shoot, that's all.'

Now she'd said it, she was concerned. She hadn't heard from Abel since being back home and hoped he would have something for her soon. The photo shoots topped up her income nicely. Now that her mother was staying and she wasn't getting Alessandro's weekly rent, she could do with some extra money coming in.

'I could increase my rent, if you like,' Jack offered, obviously sensing the reason behind her concern.

'No, Jack,' she said with a scowl. 'You pay your fair share and anyway, you're not really in a position to be overly generous. Not now you're soon to be out of work.'

He stood up and came over. 'Give me a hug,' he said, stretching out his arms. 'Come on,' he insisted when she didn't make a move. 'I think we could both do with one right now.'

Jack's hugs were her favourite defence against her woes. She stepped into his arms without further hesitation, breathing in his warm soapy scent. 'You showered.'

He smiled down at her. 'You say that as if it's a rare occurrence.'

Bella pinched his side making him flinch and laugh. 'I didn't mean that and you know it.'

He darted away from her. 'Hey, stop that. I'm glad you approve of my smell.'

'All I said was that you'd showered.'

She enjoyed the banter she shared with Jack. Maybe it was just as well that they were nothing more than friends, she mused. If the connection between them changed, she would miss this comfortable way they had between them. What if they got together and it didn't work out. It could change everything. Even her friendship with Sacha. She didn't want that to happen. Though would it really have to alter? she couldn't help wondering.

She realised Jack was speaking. 'Sorry, you said something?'

'I was saying, you mustn't worry and that we'll make a plan.'

She smiled at the familiar words. 'You've picked that up from my mum, haven't you? She's always saying the same thing.'

'She's a wise lady.'

Bella wasn't so sure about that. 'Sometimes, I suppose.'

'Anyway, I might have a job.'

Bella stepped back. 'Really? Where?'

He shook his head, hands on his hips as he frowned. 'Hey, don't sound so shocked. I'm not completely unemployable, you know?'

She giggled. 'Who are you going to be working for?'

'Tony.'

'Fisherman, Tony?' She wasn't sure she liked this idea too much. 'But you'll go out in all weathers. It could be dangerous.'

Jack's expression softened and all his amusement vanished. 'Will you worry about me?'

She pushed his right shoulder, hard. 'Of course I'll bloody worry about you,' she said, before she had time to think. Then, embarrassed to have been so open with her feelings, she added, 'And so will Sacha. I'm sure she'll have something to say about you going out to sea each day.'

She walked into the kitchen to give her something to do.

Jack followed. 'I'm a big boy now.'

'I know.' She squeezed her eyes closed, relieved he was behind her and couldn't see her battling to suppress her feelings.

'Then you'll also know that I don't need anyone's permission.' He turned and marched out of the room. 'Shit. What is it about the women around me?' she heard him grumble as he went up the stairs. 'You all think you've got a right to tell me what to do.'

Bella leant against the worktop, her head drooping. Why couldn't she think before she spoke? He was right though; he could think for himself and no doubt he would do so when Nicki unveiled her plans for their wedding. The thought calmed her slightly. She needed to focus on her own troubles and leave Jack to get on with what he needed to do. What was wrong with being a fisherman anyway?

'It's bloody dangerous, that's what,' she mumbled, switching on the kettle.

'What is?' her mother whispered behind her, giving her a fright and making her wallop her elbow on the corner of the cooker as she spun around.

'Don't creep up on me like that,' Bella snapped.

'You haven't answered my question.'

Bella rubbed the pain away and pointed upstairs, putting a finger to her lips. 'Shush, I don't want Jack to hear.'

'What?'

She told her about his job offer.

Claire thought for a moment. 'I don't know what the problem is. He respects the water and let's face it, knows how to deal with it far better than most of us. He'll be fine. Be happy for him that his money problems are solved.'

She was probably right, Bella thought. It was none of her business anyway what Jack did, more's the pity.

Her mother was about to add something just as Bella's phone rang. She pulled it out of her pocket. It was Abel. Relieved at the prospect of another photo shoot, she answered.

'Hi,' she said cheerfully. 'And the answer is yes.'

There was a hesitation before he said, 'You don't know the question yet. I'm, er, not phoning about a shoot. I need you to do me a favour. To be honest, I need you to do one for my girlfriend.'

'I'd be delighted to,' she said, trying to imagine what she could possibly be able to do. 'What is it?'

She heard a muffled comment and presumed he had placed his hand over the receiver so she couldn't hear what was being said.

'I need you to find somewhere for Megan to stay.'

She might be willing to put herself out for a job, but having that little madam staying with her was not something she'd even contemplate. 'If you're referring to Megan Knight, then I'm afraid the answer has to be a resounding no.'

He sighed heavily. 'I knew that would be your first answer.'

'And my final one,' she snapped, irritated with him for asking.

'Look, I know she's a nightmare.'

'That's an understatement. Abel, she's been famous for what, a month? How does anyone have such a high opinion of themselves after being in the public eye for only that length of time? I don't get it.'

'Bella, babes.'

'Don't call me that, Abel,' she said through gritted teeth. 'Especially if you want something from me.'

'No, of course, that was silly of me. Sorry. She's Megan's agent and is expecting me to help her sort something out.' He sounded flustered, and if Bella was right, his girlfriend was in the background, giving him a hard time. Someone was, and it didn't sound like Megan. 'Please, Bella. I'm desperate. She's had a fling with this financier bloke. He's got a reputation for being a bad boy and her manager has managed to sign her up for an exclusive with one of the big gossip magazines. We need somewhere for her to lie low where she can't get into trouble.'

'We do have the Internet here, you know,' she said, indignant that he was making her home sound like some backwater. 'We all use mobile phones here. I don't see how her being on the island is going to keep her from making trouble.'

'We have a better chance of her not being found if she's there though,' he said. 'You're used to celebrities being over there on Jersey.'

'We say *in* Jersey, actually. And we're more used to people who've done something to become famous than the five-minute celebs like Megan.'

He groaned. 'Are you going to help me with this, or not.'

'No.' There, she'd said it. Relieved, Bella smiled at her mum for the first time that day.

'Pulease, Bella.'

Bugger. He wasn't going to give up, Bella thought, her mood dropping again. 'Why should I?'

'Come on, Bella,' he pleaded in a singsong voice that wasn't nearly as enticing as he probably imagined it to be. 'I'll never ask anything of you again. I'll make sure you go to the top of my list of hand models in the future, too.'

'For this you'd better,' she said, the thought of further lucrative work from him helping to lower her resolve. 'Anyway, where am I supposed to put her? My cottage is already full and...' She was about to add that she had no idea where Megan could stay, when he spoke.

'We'll pay you, very well. It's just for a few days. A week, tops.'

She realised that this could help Lexi out. Her cottages were almost certainly empty at this time of year, and both she and her friend needed extra cash. She pretended to consider his offer. 'I'm not sure. How much were you willing to pay?'

He named a figure, then before she could answer, doubled it.

'I'll have to get back to you with the cost of the accommodation,' she said. 'If Megan wants to be inconspicuous, then you'll need to ensure the other two cottages are kept empty.'

'You're a hard taskmaster to have, Bella. Do you know that?' He sounded relieved and amused by her bartering with him.

'Fine. Give me an hour to see what I can do and I'll call you back. When would she be arriving?'

'Private plane, 10 a.m. tomorrow.'

She could hear the smile in his voice. He must have given some indication to his girlfriend, who she had discovered was also Megan's agent, that Bella had agreed because there was a loud triumphant whoop in the background.

She ended the call and grabbed her coat. 'Won't be long, Mum,' she said as she ran out of the door.

* * *

'Who?' Lexi asked, looking as confused as Bella expected someone who didn't read magazines or watch television to look.

'She's the latest reality TV star to hit the papers,' she explained. 'She was in a series called *Love 'Em or Leave 'Em*. I never watched it, but Betty loves it. Apparently, the contest—'

'I don't care,' Lexi broke in. 'I'm not having one of those weirdos staying at my cottages.'

She didn't like to ask how Lexi could be so against Megan if she hadn't even watched her on television. 'They're full then?' she asked, knowing they weren't. Lexi shook her head slowly, her short, black pixie haircut making her look nineteen, rather than twenty-nine. 'And don't tell me you couldn't do with the cash.'

'Why's he paying you, if the girl is staying with me?'

'Because I'm locating somewhere for her to stay. A sort of finder's fee, if you like.'

Lexi widened her eyes. 'Hah, good for you. But, if she's any trouble you can come and sort her out.'

Relieved to have good news for Abel, Bella hugged her friend. 'Thanks, Lex. I owe you one.'

'Don't be daft. You've done me a favour. Tell me what you know about her.'

'I will,' said Bella. 'And I'll tell you what I need you to do when she gets to Jersey.'

* * *

The following morning at 10.15 a.m., a car with blacked out windows dropped Megan at the fisherman's cottages. Bella thought the least she could do for her friend was wait with her for Megan to arrive, and introduce them. She glanced at Lexi and could see that her friend was as anxious as she was to see how the next few days would pan out.

The driver parked the car and got out. He opened the rear door nearest Lexi and Bella and for a few seconds nothing happened. Bella wondered if maybe Megan had changed her mind about coming, but then reasoned that the driver wouldn't have wasted his time coming here, if she had.

Eventually, a long spray-tanned leg appeared, followed by another one, and then the woman they'd both been waiting for.

'She must have a month's worth of make-up on and that's just her legs,' Lexi whispered. 'If she's supposed to be incognito, why all the slap?'

'Shush, we're supposed to be greeting her, not judging her,' Bella said, wondering whether she'd done the right thing by agreeing to let Megan stay at the cottages.

'I'm guessing not much happens around here,' Megan said, pouting as she gazed at the three white-painted buildings before turning her back on them to look at the view. She appeared not to recognise Bella. 'What's down there?' she asked, pointing towards the sea and the boardwalk running along in front of it.

Bella explained. 'I live down there, in the blue cottage called The Bee Hive. There's also the Summer Sundaes Beach Café, run by our friend Sacha, and the Isola Bella *gelateria* run by her boyfriend.'

'Hmm.'

Lexi stepped forward, her hand outstretched. 'Hi, I'm Lexi,' she said. 'These are my cottages and they're all vacant, so you won't be disturbed. I've made the middle one up for you.'

Megan ignored her outstretched hand and glared at the driver as he unloaded two huge suitcases, a smaller case and a designer handbag. 'I suppose I'm stuck here now,' she said, as he reversed the car onto the hill and drove away at speed.

'It's not so bad,' Lexi said, frowning. 'There's wood for the log burner, so you'll be nice and warm in the cottage and there's a TV in there, too.'

Megan stared at her as if she was an idiot.

A spot of rain landed on Bella's forehead. 'Come along,' she said, waving for Megan to follow. 'Let's get your things inside.' She began dragging the first case into the cottage and Lexi followed with the second one. 'Er, you can bring the rest of your stuff unless you want it to get wet.'

Lexi gave Bella a meaningful glance as they entered the cottage. 'I foresee fun ahead,' she said, not bothering to hide her dislike of her new guest.

Megan stomped in behind them, slamming her smaller case down in the tiny hallway. 'How the hell am I supposed to stay here for the next few days? There is literally like nothing to do.'

Not wishing Lexi to get irritated and tell Megan to bugger off, Bella smiled and tried to jolly the other two along. 'Let's get your cases upstairs and then we can see about finding a way to keep you entertained.'

Two minutes later, as they struggled into the bedroom, there was a knock at the door.

'They can't have discovered me here already, surely?' Megan appeared delighted at the prospect. 'What will I say to them?'

Bella wasn't sure who 'they' were, but went to find out. Lexi blocked the doorway. 'No, it's fine. You stay here and help your friend. I'll see who it is.'

Hearing Jack's deep voice downstairs, Bella's mood immediately lifted.

'Ooh, who's that?' Megan asked, leaving the room without waiting for Bella to reply. 'Hi, my name's Megan,' Bella heard her saying seconds later, in a flirtatious tone.

By the time she'd reached the bottom of the stairs, Megan already had Jack's right hand in a vice-like grip and was kissing him on the cheek. She seemed much happier.

Jack looked over her blonde head at Bella. 'Your mum said you were up here and I needed to ask you something.' He moved away from Megan, only for her to stand next to him again.

'Looks like it might not be so boring, after all,' she said, looking up at him under her false eyelashes.

Jack looked confused. 'Er, Bella? Can I have a quick word?'

Amused to be the one rescuing him, she followed him outside. 'What's the matter?'

'Was that what's her name? From the papers? From the dating show?'

'Yes, yes and yes.'

'Why is she in Lexi's cottage?'

Bella explained about Abel's call for help. 'It's helping Lexi and me out of a tight spot financially,' she said. 'Mind you, I think we're both going to have to work for it.'

'You could be right. She looks a right handful. Um, that is...'

Bella laughed. 'It's fine, I know what you mean.' She stood on tiptoes and whispered in his ear. 'You're right, she is.'

'Poor Lex.'

'Poor you, too,' she said, enjoying teasing him.

'What do you mean?'

'You're going to have to help Lexi and me entertain her.' She raised her hand to stop him arguing. 'We can't leave Lexi to do this alone. You saw what Megan's like, and you only met her for a few minutes, if that.'

He nodded. 'Fine. What do you want me to do?'

'We've got to stop her from going on social media. Her manager has arranged a hefty fee for an exclusive from her. Abel called again this morning and said that we've only got to do this until the interview tomorrow. Karina Pierce is the journalist coming to speak to Megan. She, her photographer and a stylist will be arriving with Megan's manager on the red-eye tomorrow morning. They've sent Megan here today to keep her away from the paparazzi camping out at her mum's home, where she's been staying. We can relax after that.'

'That's no problem,' he said, grinning at her.

'What?'

'I hope this is going to be as simple as you're expecting,' he said, shaking his head.

Bella frowned at him. 'It'll be fine. I'm going to ask Sacha to supply us with food and drink. Mum can come up later and take over from me and Lexi for a bit.' She caught Jack laughing quietly. 'I don't know why you're so amused, it's you she's taken a liking to, so she's going to want you here as much as possible.'

'I have my limits,' he said. 'Anyway, I promised Nicki I'd meet her in the pub later for a chat about something. She said it was important.'

Bella's cheerful mood vanished. 'Have you any idea what it could be about?'

He shook his head.

'Come along, you two,' Megan said, opening the front door and pretending to shiver. 'It's freezing out here.'

'Then I guess you won't want to come down to the boardwalk to stretch your legs for a bit?' Jack said.

'Like, yeah.'

He glanced at Bella. 'I presume we're all going?'

Not wishing to leave him to cope with Megan on her own, she zipped up her puffa jacket and smiled. 'I wouldn't miss it. You coming, Lexi?'

'No, thanks,' Lexi shouted from inside. 'I'll stay here.'

Bella didn't blame her. She opened her mouth to say something to Megan who had disappeared inside, only to be almost bowled over by her when she flung the door open and ran out. She watched as Megan linked arms with Jack and hugged him close to her.

'You'll keep me warm, won't you, Jack?' she cooed.

Jack gave her an uncertain smile and looked back to find Bella. 'You coming?' he said, reaching out for her to take hold of his hand.

Relieved that he had thought of her, she took his hand in hers and linked arms with him, too. It was a little closer than she usually got to him, but on this occasion, it somehow didn't seem odd. At least she wasn't gazing up into his eyes. That would be out of character. For her, at least.

They walked down to the boardwalk. 'I'd better pull my hood down to cover my face a bit,' Megan said. 'Don't want no one spotting me. That journalist would create merry hell if I said the wrong thing to someone before she gets here.' Bella tried to tune out while Megan rattled on about the money she was going to make and the bloke she was seeing. 'He's loaded,' she heard her say. 'And hot. Not my normal type. He's more like you, Jack.' Her voice softened once again.

'What's this man like then, Megan?' Bella asked, assuming she should at least try to be friendly to the girl. 'Where did you meet him?'

'He's a financier. Olly. Scottish, he is. Did I say he was worth a mint?'

'Yes, I think so.'

'We've only been seeing each other a week and a half, but we have a strong connection.' Bella could not imagine what they had in common. 'You know? Like you and me, Jack. I knew it as soon as our eyes met up.'

'Aw well, I'll have to be sure I don't upset your boyfriend then, won't I?' Jack said, sounding relieved.

'What he doesn't know, and all that,' Megan giggled. Jack glanced at Bella. 'Come on, show me this beach of yours then,' Megan said.

They reached the railings. Bella breathed in the cold, salty air, relishing the freshness. 'I never get tired of this place.'

Megan looked as if she'd smelt something rotten. 'I can see

why it would be fun here in the summer, but it's wet and nasty today. What is there to do?'

'Jack surfs,' Bella said. 'Don't you?' She nudged him slightly.

'Yes. The tide is too messy for surfing today. But when the waves are large, it's incredible.'

'That's a shame, I wouldn't mind you giving me a surfing lesson. In the summer when it's hot, though. I can't see myself in a bikini in weather like this,' Megan said, glowering at the breaking waves and squawking seagulls.

'Never mind,' Jack said, widening his eyes at Bella, in relief.

'Shall we walk on the beach?' Bella asked.

'Nah, you're all right. Why don't we go back up to the cottages and have something bubbly?'

It was better than nothing, Bella thought. 'I'm not sure Lexi has anything bubbly in the fridge, but I can go and see if Sacha has a bottle of anything at the café, if you like?'

'Go on then. Jack and I will meet you when you get back. You can sort out some food for us too, while you're at it.'

Irritated by Megan's rudeness, and assumption that she was going to be at her beck and call the entire time she was on the island, Bella bit her tongue. She was relieved to have time away from the ghastly girl and was careful not to look at Jack as she turned to leave them.

Sacha was behind the counter when Bella entered the café. 'That's the dreaded Megan, I presume?' she whispered.

'It is,' said Bella. 'She's horrible, but it's not for long.'

'It's still too long by the look on Jack's face,' Sacha giggled. 'Is there anything I can do to help?'

Bella asked about some food and was delighted when Sacha brought out two bottles of champagne for her to take up to the cottage.

'Lexi needs all the help she can get to keep money coming in,' she said. 'Things have gone downhill since her father was rude to some of his returning visitors.'

'I heard about that a few weeks ago,' said Bella. 'Maybe you can come up to the cottage later, when you've closed the café?'

'Will do. I can't wait to meet Megan. I watched that show, mainly to see what she got up to next. She was really entertaining,' Sacha said. 'Mind you, it's one thing watching someone on the telly, but another dealing with them in real life.'

Bella thought back to the half an hour she'd spent watching the first episode with Sacha. 'You're not kidding,' she said, helping to pack two quiches, some salad, a cabbage loaf and the bottles of champagne in two baskets. 'Blimey, these weigh a ton.'

'I can bring one of them over later,' Sacha said. 'It'll give me a reason to come up without looking like I'm inviting myself.'

'Bring my mum with you, if she wonders where I am, will you?' Bella didn't want her mother to be left with nothing to do.

She thanked Sacha and made her way up the hill to the cottages. Reaching the front door, red-faced and hot after the exertion of carrying the baskets, she took a moment to compose herself.

Pressing the door handle awkwardly with her elbow, she could hear Nicki's high-pitched voice arguing with Megan. She groaned quietly and walked in.

'Listen to me, you little madam,' Nicki shouted, pointing a manicured nail centimetres from Megan's nose. 'If I want to speak to my boyfriend, I don't need your bloody permission to do so.'

'Shuuuut uppp,' Lexi bellowed. 'That's enough of the pair of you. This is my cottage. If you have an issue with Megan, who is my guest, then you need to be the one to leave.'

Bella pushed open the door into the open plan living room with its tiny kitchen area. 'Supplies,' she shouted, trying to distract them from their argument. She pushed the door closed with her bottom.

'Oh, it's you.' Nicki sneered at her, eyes narrowed.

That wasn't the reaction Bella had been hoping for. She glanced at Lexi, who hurried towards her relieving her of one of the baskets. 'Champagne!' she blew a kiss at Bella. 'You've no idea how much I'm going to enjoy this.'

'I think I have,' Bella whispered, lifting her basket onto the small kitchen counter and starting to unpack. Lifting out a cabbage loaf, she turned and caught Nicki still staring at her. She looked as if she was waiting for a reaction. 'Sorry, Nicki,' she said, continuing to take out the rest of the produce. 'You seemed to be irritated with me for some reason.'

'Well, you're the one who brought her here.' She pointed over her shoulder at Megan, who was glaring at Nicki's back, arms folded across her chest. 'She's been on the television for what, a couple of hours at most, and acts like she's some sort of diva.'

Bella stopped what she was doing. 'I'm sorry, I had no idea you even knew Megan, let alone that you two have some sort of issue with each other.'

'I don't know that cow,' Megan said without moving.

Which was probably a good thing, Bella mused, as the room seemed rather full with the five of them in it. 'Okay, so why all the drama then?'

'I caught her getting off with Jack.'

Bella stopped what she was doing, her heart constricting with... what? Envy, jealousy, or was it simply disappointment in Jack? She certainly couldn't blame Megan, especially as he was single, whatever Nicki was insinuating.

Bella cleared her throat and took the brownies Sacha had packed for them out of the basket without turning to face the others.

'When did this happen? I've only been gone half an hour and Megan hasn't been here very long.'

Megan pushed past Nicki and then Bella and flounced out of the living room and up the stairs, shouting, 'Why won't you listen to me? Nothing happened.'

'She's a bloody liar,' Nicki snapped. 'I know what I saw. If I hadn't been walking up from the boardwalk, I wouldn't have seen them all over each other, on the doorstep.'

Lexi put everything away in the two small cupboards. 'Nicki, whatever you saw, you aren't seeing Jack any more, so I really don't understand what it's got to do with you, or why you think you've got the right to barge into one of my cottages and shout at my guest.' She walked to the front door and opened it, waving for Nicki to leave. 'I think it's time you left Megan to settle in, don't you?'

Recalling that Megan's visit was supposed to be a secret until after the interview, Bella ran to join them and explained. 'Please keep her visit to yourself, won't you?'

Nicki shook her head. 'I'll do what I damn well choose.'

Bella and Lexi stood on the doorstep and watched Nicki marching down the hill towards the hotel.

'Bugger,' Bella said. 'I have a feeling that Megan's secret visit will soon be common knowledge.'

'So do I.'

Bella sighed. 'Don't worry, I'll go and see if Megan's okay. I know she's a bit of a pain, but Nicki can be fierce, and she didn't deserve an attack like that.'

She decided it was her responsibility to soothe any bruised egos. She was the one who had got them all involved in the magazine-shoot issues. She reached Megan's bedroom and knocked lightly on the door. 'Megan, are you okay?'

Hearing sobbing, Bella opened the door slowly and peered

into the room. Megan was sitting on the bed, stifling her sobs with the pillow.

She spotted Bella and threw the pillow behind her, wiping at her eyes. 'What are you doing in here?'

'I knocked first,' Bella said, surprised to see the younger girl hurrying to hide her distress. 'Nicki's gone now. Why don't you come downstairs? It's only Lexi and me down there now.' She took a clean tissue from the box on the small dressing table and handed it to Megan.

She blew her nose before standing up to check her reflection in the mirror. 'I look horrendous.'

Bella didn't like to agree, but her cheeks were awash with mascara. 'Take a few minutes to sort yourself out and I'll open one of those bottles of bubbly.'

'It's only lunchtime, too. You do live dangerously on this island.'

Her sarcasm didn't worry Bella. 'Only occasionally.' Her glimpse into Megan's fragility had surprised her. Maybe there was more to this defensive girl, after all. She didn't like the fact that she had been so quick to judge Megan as hard and unfeeling. 'I'll see you downstairs then.'

'How is she?' Lexi asked when Bella joined her in the kitchenette.

'Crying like she's heartbroken. It was upsetting to see.'

Lexi took the cabbage loaf out of its white paper bag and slammed it onto the counter. 'I think you need to have a word with Nicki, or I can. She's very quick to assume we all want what she's got.' Bella didn't reply. 'You okay?'

She nodded. 'I think I might have misjudged Megan, you know?'

Lexi stared at her briefly. 'I think you're overtired or something. Now, help me make some sandwiches. I don't want this loaf to go to waste.' She cut neat slices and handed them to Bella to butter. 'I thought ham and a few cheese and tomato.'

Bella vaguely heard her speaking and did as she suggested, but couldn't get the sight of Megan out of her mind. 'I think that maybe Jack should be the one to approach Nicki about what happened today. After all, he is her ex and was the one supposedly caught kissing Megan. He should be the one to put things right.'

'I agree,' Lexi said, washing and drying the knife before putting it back into the drawer. 'She doesn't seem to like you much anyway, so I doubt she'll entertain anything you've got to say.'

'True.' Bella placed the sandwiches on a plate and took three smaller ones from the cupboard overhead. 'Though I'm not sure why she's so odd with me. It's not as if I've been caught kissing Jack.' More's the pity, she thought.

'She probably doesn't like your closeness,' Lexi said, grabbing three champagne glasses. 'You two are like little besties nowadays.'

They both looked up as Megan entered the room. Bella couldn't believe how immaculate she looked. Her eyes weren't even puffy. It was as if she'd imagined it all.

She caught Lexi looking at her questioningly as she placed a tea towel over the top of the champagne bottle, gripping it tightly as she turned it, until the cork was released with a popping sound.

'Are you feeling better?' Bella asked Megan.

'I'm fine now. She took me by surprise, that's all.' She gave a brief smile. 'I didn't, you know.'

'What?'

'Kiss Jack.' She waited while Lexi poured the champagne into the glasses and took one. 'Thanks.' Turning her attention back to

Bella, she added, 'I don't care what that cow thinks of me, but you've been kind to me and I didn't want you to think that I had.'

Bella was relieved to hear it. 'Let's get comfortable and make the most of this lovely champagne.'

After several minutes enjoying their extra special lunch, Megan said, 'I want to apologise for being such a bitch at the photo shoot. I know it's no excuse, but I'm exhausted since coming off the show. My manager said that I have to make the most of my fifteen minutes of fame, so she's accepting everything that's being offered to me. It makes sense, I suppose, but I've been desperate for some time away from it all.'

Bella could see now how vulnerable Megan was. She was nothing more than a frightened girl, trying not to miss any opportunity that came her way.

'Then why not treat this brief stay on the island as a mini break? It's peaceful here.' She laughed. 'When you haven't got visitors and people giving you a hard time.'

'Yes, we'll show you around a bit but let you have a lie in and catch up with some sleep,' Lexi said, wiping her mouth with a sheet of kitchen roll. 'I'm staying next door at the moment,' she said, pointing in the direction of the cottage on the left. 'I'll do my best to ensure you're left alone when you want to be and you can always come to mine for a chat, if Bella is working.'

'That's so kind,' Megan said, her eyes welling up again.

'I didn't mean to upset you,' Lexi said, taking Megan's empty glass and refilling it. She widened her eyes at Bella.

Unsure what to do, Bella cleared her throat. It occurred to her that maybe Megan was missing her family, or lonely without any familiar people around her. 'I know we didn't get off to the best of starts but you are with friends here. We'll look out for you, if that's what's bothering you.'

'You don't understand,' Megan sniffed. 'Since being out of the programme it's like everyone I meet wants a piece of me. It's been horrible and not at all like I expected being a celeb would be. You two, and Jack, have been the first people to be kind to me and not want something back.'

Surprised to hear her being so open, Bella smiled. 'That's good to know. Well, not the bit about everyone being horrible, but the bit about us.'

'Yes,' agreed Lexi. 'Treat this place like your home while you're here and chill.'

There was a knock on the door.

Megan stood up. 'I'll get it. If it's that Nicki, I'll give her a mouthful.' She smiled at the others. 'I'm feeling much better now.' She walked to the door and opened it.

'Is Bella here?'

Recognising her mother's voice, Bella shouted, 'It's okay, you can let her in!'

'I'm her mother,' she heard Claire say to Megan. 'Sorry to barge in, but I—' She gazed around the cramped living room. 'Am I missing a party?'

'No, Mum. Anyway, why are you here?' After all she had said to Megan, she didn't want her thinking that the entire village was going to invite themselves to the cottage.

'You're Bella's mum? That's amazing,' Megan said, shaking her hand.

There was another knock. 'I wonder who this is?' Megan said, grinning as she went to answer it.

'Sorry, we didn't mean for your stay to be like this,' Lexi said, pulling a face at Bella.

'It's fine. This is like being back at home with my family, I like it.' They waited as she opened the door. 'Oh, it's you.'

By the flirtatious tone of her voice, Bella assumed it was Jack. She was right.

'Hi, I was... bloody hell, am I missing a party?'

'No,' Lexi and Bella said in unison.

'We've finished the first bottle,' Lexi said. 'We thought we should keep the second one for later, in case Sacha joined us.'

Jack grinned. 'I wasn't hinting about the booze. I came to tell you that Nicki found me and gave me a mouthful about, well, about you,' he said to Megan. 'I wanted you to know that I've put her straight. There's no need to worry about it happening again. I'm sorry about that,' he said. 'She can be a bit overbearing sometimes.'

'I'd call it ignorant and rude,' Megan replied, showing the side of her that Bella recognised best. 'I hope she's going to apologise.'

'I told her she should, but I wouldn't hold your breath. I'll do it on her behalf.'

'Thank you,' Megan said, sounding genuinely pleased.

'Right, I'd better go. Nicki said she had something she needed to discuss with me and, as much as I'd rather stay here and chat to you all, I'd better go. Otherwise, she'll probably come up here looking for me again and I doubt any of you want that.'

'No, we don't.' Lexi laughed.

'Have I missed something?' Claire asked.

Someone's mobile rang. After a moment where the four of them checked their phones, Megan stood up and waved her mobile in the air. 'My manager,' she said, leaving the room and going back upstairs.

'I'll tidy this lot. You can get off if you like, Bella,' Lexi said. 'I'm sure you have loads to get on with. We can always meet back here later. I'll check with Megan what she wants to do when she's off the phone and let you know.'

'Great. Come along then, Mum,' said Bella. 'You sure you don't want me to help wash up?'

'No, you two get on.'

Bella and Claire shivered as they stepped outside, both doing up their jackets and pushing their hands deep into their pockets.

'It's freezing,' Claire grumbled as they began walking down to the boardwalk.

'Almost,' Bella said. She couldn't stop worrying about Jack and wondered if Nicki was going to tell him about her wedding plans. She should have pre-warned him. Why hadn't she gone with her gut instinct and done so?

'What's the matter with you?' Claire asked, linking arms with her. 'You look very pensive today. 'Is it something I can help you with?'

Bella shook her head. 'It's nothing, don't worry.'

Claire pulled her to a stop and studied her face. 'I know there's something troubling you.'

'It's a secret,' she said, aware that her mother wouldn't give up until she said something. 'I've been sworn to secrecy.'

'What did you promise exactly?'

'Mum, it's nothing and I'm fine. Honestly.'

Bella tugged Claire's arm gently, forcing her mum to continue walking with her.

'You do know that it helps to share a problem.'

'There's no problem,' she said, tired of the questioning. 'At least not for me.'

Claire pulled her to a stop again.

'Mum, I can't tell you, so leave it. Please.'

'No, I won't. You're worrying me. I won't drop the matter until I know what's going on.'

Bella sighed. She knew when she was beaten. 'Fine, but you've got to promise not to tell anyone. Okay?'

'Cross my heart,' she said, winking at Bella triumphantly.

'Who knows, I might already have been told whatever it is that's worrying you.'

'I doubt it.' Bella shivered. 'I'll tell you while we walk home.' She proceeded to tell her mother everything that Jools' grandmother had overheard. It wasn't easy. She hated betraying a confidence, but in this case, she held no loyalty to Nicki and did care, very much, that Jack was being lied to.

'What do you think?' she asked, after giving her mother time to contemplate what she'd told her. 'Should I tell Jack?'

'Do you want to?'

'Yes.'

'Then do it.'

11

The sun didn't seem to be out when Bella woke the following morning. A familiar dread swept over her, that only those who lived on an island would understand.

'Please no,' she whispered, getting out of bed and pulling open her curtains. She peered at the dense veil of fog shrouding the boardwalk and knew the airport would be closed. 'Bugger.' She groaned. 'No planes in or out of the island today.' This would delay the photo shoot and Megan's return to the mainland. Bella assumed that the interview could take place via a conference call, or online. Aware that if Lexi hadn't broken the news to the girl, then she would have to, Bella's mood dipped. She didn't relish the thought and took her mind off the prospect by showering and dressing.

She went to find Jack downstairs, hoping to have a word with him before he went out. It occurred to her that she hadn't seen him since he had left to speak to Nicki the previous day. If he had come home at all, it must have been late because she hadn't heard him, which was unusual. She pushed aside the thought that he most probably had spent the night with Nicki. It wasn't her place to have an opinion on what he did, she thought miserably.

Her mother was still asleep. Wanting to delay the moment she had to speak to Megan, and to take her mind off what Jack might be doing with Nicki, Bella decided to pay Betty a visit. She put on her jacket and stepped outside. It was only just eight in the morning, but she knew her elderly neighbour would be up and about. Bella crossed the boardwalk and leant on the cool iron railings, sticky with salt from the stormy waves that had lashed them during the night.

No one was about and, with the fog resting on the sea, it seemed as if the village was an island itself. There was a peacefulness at times like this, which Bella loved. The fog enveloped the village like a duvet, masking the sounds of cars on the nearby road and the distant roar of jets taking off from the airport a couple of miles away. The only sound came from the waves lapping against the bottom of the sea wall, and everything was calm.

She turned left to continue on her way to Betty's and spotted some frosted glass on the beach. The pretty colours were displayed in the same symbol that had adorned the boardwalk during the summer. She crouched down to get a better look. They were arranged on the sea wall, between the railings and the beach, and must have been done early that morning before everyone was up. Intrigued, Bella hoped that one day someone would discover who was responsible and what the symbols meant. They were obviously important to someone, but who?

Hurrying to Betty's, she knocked on the front door.

'Come in, love,' the old lady called, her voice sounding slightly weaker than usual.

She was sitting in her favourite chair overlooking the waves, and Bella walked over and kissed her on the cheek.

'How are you?' Betty asked, motioning for her to sit on the chair opposite. 'Your mum driving you mad yet?'

Bella laughed. 'No, she's been fine. I've enjoyed having her at the cottage to be honest,' she admitted.

'Not really fair on young Alessandro, having to move out though, is it?' Betty said sagely. 'Given any indication of how long she'll be stopping here, has she?'

'No, none.' Bella wondered if her mother had already begun making plans to leave and hadn't liked to tell her. She hoped not. She was enjoying catching up with her too much to be ready to say good-bye just yet.

'Hmm.' Betty studied Bella's face.

Bella smiled, wanting to reassure her friend. 'It's fine, honestly. I don't think he minds that much.' She had been wondering if Alessandro and Sacha might see this as an opportunity for him to move into her flat above the café, but nothing had happened so far.

'And your Jack. How's he doing with that nasty piece back on the rock?'

'He's not my Jack.' Bella wished Betty wouldn't stare at her so intently. 'I've no idea about him and Nicki. The last I saw of him he was going to visit her.'

Betty tapped her walking stick on the leg of a nearby coffee table. 'That shelf under there, get the brochure for me, will you?'

Bella bent down, and finding what she assumed Betty wanted, handed it to her. 'What is it?'

'She was in Sacha's café the other day and this fell out of her bag.' She waved the leaflet in the air. 'Have a read. Go on. Tell me what you make of it.'

It was a prospectus for a development company. Bella opened it, intrigued.

'They're looking for properties on the island with sea views.'

It didn't make any sense. 'She's in finance though, not property. Why would she be interested in this, do you think?'

Betty stared at her for a moment. 'Finder's fee, that's what Claire reckons.'

'You've shown this to my mum? She never said anything.'

Betty frowned. 'Why would she?'

She had a point. Bella had been so focused on Megan, and she and her mum had more than enough to chat about since her return without needing to discuss Nicki's antics. 'I'm sure it's nothing,' Bella said, hoping to reassure Betty. 'It could be something she picked up somewhere or was given. Who knows?' She changed the subject. 'I really want to know how you are now the weather's turned?'

'A bit dodgy on my feet, my love, but fine apart from that. My rheumatism plays me up a bit in this damper weather but I've got nothing to complain about.'

'Good. You must let me know if there is anything I can get you, or do for you.'

Betty smiled. 'Jack's always checking on me and bringing me things that I need. He takes me for breakfast, too. That's how I caught up with all Claire's news.'

'Of course.' Remembering the date, and what Betty had had to deal with the previous year, she said, 'It's Halloween today. If you get any of those little sods throwing eggs at your windows, you let one of us know, won't you?'

'Yes. Tony, the fisherman, has already spoken to me. He only lives down the way and he'll sort the little devils out if they make a mess of the place.'

It occurred to Bella that most people Betty's age would be nervous to live alone with kids trashing their place. As she spotted Jack walking past the window, her stomach did a flip and she focused on remaining composed.

'Here's young Jack now,' Betty said, beaming from ear to ear as he entered the room. 'Good morning, lad,' she called. 'How are you with all that's going on?'

He frowned. 'Nothing much going on in my world,' he said, glancing at Bella quizzically. 'Not that I'm aware of.'

'Why, what have you heard?' Bella asked the older lady. She knew that nothing much passed her by, and with most of the neighbours paying her visits throughout the week, Betty didn't have to walk far to know exactly what was happening in the village.

The older lady shrugged her skinny shoulders. 'I couldn't possibly say.'

'Has Mum been talking to you?' Bella asked without thinking. As soon as the words were out of her mouth, she cringed. 'That is to say...'

Jack folded his arms across his chest. 'Hang on a sec,' he said, staring at Bella intently. 'What does your mum know about me that I don't? Come on, tell me.'

She desperately wanted to, but prided herself on never breaking a confidence.

'Bella?' All amusement in his navy-blue eyes disappeared.

If her mum had already told Betty, then she would no doubt have told her best friend – Jack's Aunt Rosie. Everyone knew Rosie was incapable of keeping a secret.

Bella tried to work out how best to tell him. Then, remembering how good a friend he'd always been to her, especially lately, helping her with the autumn market and delivering stock to her customers, she said, 'Nicki's planning a secret wedding for you.'

Betty dropped her walking stick. Jack stared at Bella for a split second before picking up the stick and handing it back to the older lady.

'Why?' he asked, looking dumbfounded at the news.

'I don't know. Because she wants to marry you, presumably,' she said, confused by his question.

Jack's mouth slowly drew back into a smile and then he began to laugh.

Shocked, Bella exchanged glances with Betty, who looked as surprised as she was by his reaction.

'I thought Mum had told you,' she said.

'Not about that, lovey,' said Betty. 'I thought you were going to tell him about that actress who's staying up at one of Lexi's cottages on the hill.'

Irritated with herself for reacting without thinking things through, Bella groaned. 'No, Jack already knew that news. And she's not an actress, she's a reality star.'

Remembering the fog, and Megan's predicament, Bella stood up to leave. Hearing Jack's quiet laughter, she turned to see him wiping his eyes. Annoyed with him for not taking her seriously, she added, 'I don't know what's so funny about a surprise wedding. Anyone would think you liked the idea.'

His laughter stopped. 'I can't think of anything worse, to be honest,' he said. 'I suspect you probably misunderstood what you heard. We're not even dating, so I doubt Nicki would waste her time planning a wedding for us. It doesn't make sense.' He shook his head. 'Who told you, anyway?'

'I'd rather not say.'

He narrowed his eyes, amusement twinkling from them. 'Are they a reliable source?'

Why wasn't he worried about this? she wondered. 'I thoughts so, or I wouldn't have believed it. What are you going to do about it?'

'Nothing. It's supposed to be a secret.' He shook his head. She could see he thought the whole thing was ridiculous and wasn't taking it seriously. 'I'll wait and see if it turns out to be anything and deal with it then if I need to,' he said.

'Good idea, lad.' Betty coughed. 'What are you doing here anyway?'

'I promised to take you and Claire for a fry-up at Sacha's this morning, remember?'

Betty waved at him to help her stand. 'I do now.'

'I'll leave you both to it,' Bella said, kissing Betty on the cheek and zipping up her jacket before going to the door. Jack might say that he and Nicki were finished, but he always seemed to jump whenever she told him to. Bella couldn't help wondering if they would ever truly be finished. There was no way she would ever entertain a relationship with someone who was still in love with, or at least closely connected to, his ex-girlfriend. And that's exactly what Jack appeared to be.

'Are you hungry?' Jack asked, interrupting her thoughts.

'What?'

'You seem deep in thought and I wondered if maybe you wanted to join us?'

'I'd love to,' she said honestly, relieved he didn't have a clue about her thought processes. 'But I've got to go and break the news to Megan that there's little chance any flights will be coming in today. The magazine crew for the photo shoot and interview will have to wait until the fog lifts before coming in, unless they can get here on the ferry.'

'And when the flights are cancelled that's usually booked quickly.'

'She wants to hope that this fog doesn't settle for the next three days,' Betty said, dolefully, handing her stick to Jack while she put on her coat. 'By the looks of it, all the planes are going to be grounded for a time yet.'

'I hope not,' Bella said, aware Betty was probably right.

'Why does it bother you so much?' Betty asked.

'Because Lexi and I have to entertain her while she's here,' Bella explained. 'Please don't tell anyone else that she's staying.'

'Why not? She's hardly Sophia Loren. I can't imagine anyone is going to be interested in her staying in the village.' Betty frowned as she concentrated on doing up her coat buttons and pulling on her gloves. 'I've never heard of the girl.'

'Why don't you invite her to the café for our small Halloween party?' Jack asked.

Bella was grateful to him for giving her something to suggest to Megan. With all the excitement of her mum's unexpected arrival, and Megan coming to the island, she had forgotten all about the event that Sacha and Alessandro had suggested to various locals.

'I can't see that she will want to join us, but I'll ask anyway.' She took a deep breath to brace herself for whatever was about to happen. 'Right, I'd better get up that hill and break the news to Megan, if Lexi hasn't already seen the fog and told her.'

'Good luck,' Jack said. 'If you need backup, you know where to find me.'

12

By the time she reached Lexi's cottage, it was obvious to Bella that Betty was wrong. The news of Megan's secret visit was already local knowledge. Bella groaned, noticing several faces she recognised, milling about, trying to look as if they were supposed to be walking up and down the hill near to the cottages.

It didn't take her long to discover that Lexi also knew.

'Bugger off,' Lexi bellowed, hands on hips, glaring at two men who seemed to be taking multiple photos with expensive looking cameras. More people seemed to be arriving by the minute, stopping to hang around to get a glimpse of Megan. 'She's not coming out,' Lexi added. 'So, there's no point in waiting.' Spotting Bella, she waved frantically at her. 'Come inside.'

Bella apologised as she gently elbowed her way through the throng outside the cottage. 'Excuse me. Nothing to see here,' she said, turning to face the crowd from the front door. 'It's freezing, so you may as well go home. Or,' she said, spotting one of the photographers shivering in an anorak that had seen better days. 'You could go to the café down on the boardwalk. Summer

Sundaes, it's called, on the right-hand side. Why not warm yourselves up with a coffee and something to eat.'

She saw him nodding and whispering to the woman next to him and left them to it. As soon as she was inside, Bella closed the door and leant against it. 'They're keen, aren't they?'

'These bloody paparazzi blokes, they've been here since I woke up. I hate to think of the pictures they've got of me looking harassed.'

'Maybe they won't use any of them,' Bella said trying her best to placate her friend.

'Yes, well I hope you're right.'

Bella followed Lexi through to the living area where a sulky Megan was slumped on one of the chairs. 'She's told you then?'

'What? That I'm bloody stuck here for at least the next twenty-four hours? What do you think?' She flicked her hair over her shoulder.

Bella sat on the arm of Lexi's chair. If Megan's intention of treating her stay in the village as a mini break had already worn off, then she'd need to find some way of keeping the girl entertained. 'It doesn't have to be that bad,' she said, hurriedly trying to think of something soothing to say. 'You must be exhausted from all the interviews since you won that competition. Why not make the most of a couple of days' peace and quiet? It'll all start up again once the magazine crew arrive for the photo shoot and interview.'

'Yeah, she's right,' Lexi said, mouthing a thank you at Bella.

Bella could only imagine how much of a drama queen Megan had been since realising she was stuck on the island.

'No,' Megan shouted. 'She's wrong. What if someone else grabs the attention of the papers while I'm here? They're only after the latest fad and I happen to be the focus of their attention at this moment in time. Or, I was, until I was persuaded to come here.' She stormed out of the room, slamming the door loudly and stomped upstairs.

'That went better than I'd expected,' Bella joked, wishing as much as Megan that the fog hadn't descended. So much for Megan's vulnerability from the night before. It was as if she was two people.

'I can see what she means,' Lexi said, standing up. She dried two coffee cups and put them away. 'She hasn't eaten anything much since she got here. I really think this is stressing her out in a big way.'

Bella hated seeing anyone in distress, but couldn't think how to help. 'Has she spoken to her manager yet?'

'About a hundred and fifty times,' Lexi groaned, hanging the tea towel over the handle on the front of the oven, which looked like it had never been used. 'She's on her way over on the next ferry, but she won't get here until tomorrow morning.'

'Is she bringing the magazine crew over with her?'

'I don't think so. Apparently, they want to fly in and out of the island on the same day, so will wait for the fog to lift.' She wiped the worktops. 'Do you think it's going to be here for the next few days?'

Bella wasn't sure whether Lexi hoped the fog would be one of the three-day visitations that the island occasionally experienced, so that she could earn more from Megan's stay, or whether she wanted her gone as soon as possible.

'Who knows?' she said. 'We're going to have to find a way to entertain her though. She'll go stir crazy if she's stuck inside all day.'

'She's not the only one,' Lexi said. 'But I daren't leave her, not if I'm being paid to take care of her.'

'We need to get her out for a walk. It might lift her spirits to do something. She'll also feel better if she eats, I know that works for me. Although with me, it's usually chocolate that cheers me up the best.'

Lexi laughed and instantly covered her mouth. 'Stop it,' she said, glancing up at the ceiling. 'I don't want her to think we're laughing about her.'

Neither did Bella. 'We'd never be that nasty.'

'She doesn't know us well enough to realise that,' Lexi said. 'What can we suggest? There are paps outside, waiting for her to come out so they can take photos.'

Bella thought for a moment. 'I know,' she said, an idea developing in her mind. She thought it through quickly, hoping her plan would work. 'I can ask my mum and Jack's Aunt Rosie to come here. Then you and Megan can swap coats and hats with them and leave.'

'Okay, well, so far this makes no sense at all,' Lexi grinned. 'Go on.'

'Mum and Rosie can pretend to be you and Megan, so that you two can leave.'

Lexi frowned. 'I can't see how this will help Megan.'

'We need to all act a little suspiciously, as if we're trying to fool the paps, but not so well that they *are* fooled. We want them to follow Megan and you.' Bella wasn't certain it was the best idea either, but it was worth a try.

'What about you?'

'I'll follow you outside with Jack.'

'Go on.'

'Stop frowning,' Bella giggled. 'This will make sense in a minute. Right, so Mum and Rosie pretend to be a diversion, but they get into your car before we speed off with Jack and Megan. We'll drive off, leading the paps on a bit of a goose chase. Then, when we get a little ahead of them, we drop Jack and Megan off for a romantic walk on the beach. They take their photos, Megan isn't forgotten, and we haven't told anyone she's staying here in the village.'

Lexi thought for a moment, a smile slowly widening on her face. 'It sort of sounds like it could work. Why not? It's not as if we have anything else to do.'

'If nothing else, it'll give us something to think about until the fog has gone.' Bella's relief vanished.

'What's the matter?'

'My mother doesn't have a mobile and I don't have Rosie's number.'

'Call Jack, he should know how to contact his aunt.'

She phoned him, her stomach doing its usual involuntary flip when she heard the sound of his deep voice. 'Hi Jack, can you get hold of your aunt and persuade her to come with my mum up to the cottage? We need them here as soon as possible. And you. Lexi and I have a clever plan.'

'I'm intrigued,' he said. 'No problem. Leave it with me.'

'Thanks, Jack,' she said, ending the call. Sensing that Lexi was watching her, she looked over at her and grinned. 'He's going to find them for us.'

'Of course he is,' Lexi said, shaking her head slowly.

Bella frowned as she slipped her phone into her back pocket. 'What's that supposed to mean?'

'I'm saying nothing,' Lexi said, taking her jacket from where it hung on a peg in the hall and removing her phone from a pocket.

'You're insinuating something though. What?'

Lexi smiled. 'It's just that your voice always changes when you're talking to Jack.'

'It does not!' *Does it?* Bella hoped Lexi was wrong.

Lexi flicked a strand of Bella's dark hair. 'I'm only teasing, but it is true. Anyway, why are you so worried about it? You like him. He's single, supposedly. I'm sure he has a thing for you, too.'

Wishing her friend was right, but knowing she wasn't, Bella argued, 'That's where you're wrong. He sees us as just friends. Anyway, until he gets Nicki well and truly out of his life, I'm staying that way.'

'You know this to be a fact, I suppose?'

Bella sighed heavily. 'Yes.'

Lexi frowned. 'Oh, sorry, Bella.'

Twenty minutes later, there was a rapid rap on the front door and Lexi rushed through. 'Those bloody paps, I wish they'd go away.' A second later, she said, 'Oh, it's you. Quick, come in.'

Bella peered into the small hallway to see who had arrived. Spotting Jack's messy fair hair, she automatically pushed her hands through her own hair. What's wrong with me? she mused. She really needed to give herself a good talking to. This infatuation with him had gone on too long and was driving her mad.

Her mother walked into the living room, closely followed by Rosie and then Jack and Lexi.

Her mother winked at her as she walked past. 'We're looking forward to getting involved in your plan.'

'Thanks, that's good of you.' She hugged her mum. 'You're freezing. Your jacket is far too light for this weather. I'll lend you one of mine.' It dawned on her that either Lexi or Megan were going to have to wear the thin jacket when they went out. 'I wish I'd thought to give you one earlier.'

'Me, too,' Lexi laughed, looking at Aunt Rosie's glamorous puffa coat. 'I can't expect my guest to get cold.'

'Sorry, I didn't expect to be swapping clothes when I came out this morning,' Claire said, smiling. 'You can wear a scarf under the jacket and some gloves, that should help relieve the cold a bit.'

Bella explained her idea to them.

'What?' Jack frowned. 'Why am I going to go on a romantic stroll with her?'

'Are you worried Nicki will find out?'

He shook his head. 'No, why?'

'Nothing,' Lexi said, looking shame-faced. 'It has to be you because you're tall and hunky and she thinks you're hot,' she explained. 'And they're not going to be interested in pictures of her with us.'

Bella was glad Lexi had been the one to explain the reasoning to Jack. 'I'll try to persuade Megan to go out, while you four work out where we should drive to.'

She walked upstairs to Megan's room and knocked on the door. 'Only me,' she said when she'd received a sullen invitation to enter. She took a deep breath and explained their proposition to the reclining girl. 'You never know, you might quite like it here.'

Megan's gaze rose from her mobile screen slowly until she was eye-to-eye with Bella. 'You think so?'

'Fine,' said Bella, not in the mood to waste her time with someone who had no intention of helping themselves. 'You stay up here and wallow. I'll go home and get on with some work.'

She turned to leave the room and Megan sat up. 'Wait, please. Sorry, I don't mean to be a cow, but I can't help panicking that they're going to forget me.'

'Then let's give them something to write about, shall we?' Bella said, as it occurred to her that the girl was genuinely frightened. She probably thought that her career was already over, and, thought Bella, it just might be. Determined to help, she said, 'We thought we could pretend we're trying to sneak out, but let them follow. If it works, then you might get photos in the papers to remind your fans you're still around. If not, then at least we've all done something to alleviate the boredom of hanging around until this fog lifts and your shoot can get underway.'

Alert to the idea, Megan looked excited for the first time since her arrival. 'Ok. We can give them a bit of a runaround and let them take some pictures.'

Relieved Megan had thought of the same idea, Bella continued, 'Why not? It should be fun.' She smiled. 'Let's go down and tell the others, shall we?'

'I love it,' Aunt Rosie said, pretending she hadn't been told the plan only minutes earlier. Bella wasn't surprised by her reaction. Jack's aunt had always enjoyed a bit of intrigue. Rosie was the most glamorous person she'd ever met and was apparently having a secret romance with a gorgeous actor who had been to the island a few times recently.

'Great,' Bella said, enthused as the plan progressed and they discussed it further.

'Are you certain you need me?' Jack asked, turning to leave.

'Yes,' Megan shouted, grabbing his arm and pulling him back into the room. 'You're my secret dalliance.'

He looked at her and grimaced. 'I'm not the only bloke living in the village, why not ask someone else?'

Bella couldn't help being amused by his disdain for the idea. 'Because you're here now and we don't have time to waste.'

'But I have things to do.'

'Like what?' Aunt Rosie asked. 'Come along. You're a hunk of a man and exactly what these celeb mags will want to write about. It makes perfect sense.'

'It does?'

'Yes,' Rosie, Bella and Lexi chorused.

'And I won't have to swap coats with you, Mum,' Bella teased. She looked at Lexi. 'Do you have a spare jacket Mum could borrow for today?'

'I'll go and get it.'

Ten minutes later, they were ready. Bella and Megan had swapped jackets and Megan wore one of Bella's bobble hats, while Bella wore one of Lexi's.

'Right,' Bella said. 'Mum and Rosie, we'll leave first. Let's go out of the back door. Make sure they see you, but act as if you're trying to be incognito.'

It was difficult not to show her amusement as she hurried out with the two older women, heads down as they hurried along the path in front of the cottages.

'Hey, ladies!' one of the paps shouted. 'Give us a smile, won't you? It's nippy as all bollocks out here.'

Claire held her hand up. 'No photos,' she said, putting her arm around Bella, as Rosie did the same. They marched off up the hill towards the park across the road.

'What are they doing?' Bella whispered.

'Two of them are taking photos,' Rosie giggled.

Bella glanced back at the cottage and noticed Jack, leading Lexi and Megan from behind the cottages.

'What's happening?' her mum asked quietly. 'Can you see if they've seen the others yet?'

'Not sure.'

Just at that moment the paps behind them stopped snapping pictures. One yelled, 'Hey, wait!' pointing at Jack and the girls, and they all turned to run after them.

Lexi unlocked her car and she, Megan and Jack, scrambled in, laughing. They drove a few yards, to where Bella, Claire and Rosie were waiting, and once they were all in the car they continued up the hill.

'Do you think they'll follow?' Megan asked, her pretty face beaming for once.

Bella turned to look. 'Yes, there are two hire cars after us.

Great. Put your foot down, Lexi. Let's at least try to appear as if we're trying to lose them.'

'I'm not going over the forty miles per hour limit,' Lexi said.

'Goody two-shoes,' Jack teased.

'You can walk if you don't like it.'

'Nah, you're all right.' Jack laughed, turning to look out of the back window at the convoy behind them. 'This is fun. Where shall we take them?'

'I think we'll make the most of the country lanes. We want them to get lost but not lose us.' Lexi changed gear and turned left.

Bella undid her window slightly to let more air into the stuffy car. Lexi's old banger was useful for lots of things, but she was aware that she needed to buy a van at some point and stop asking to borrow this vehicle. She looked out of the back window. 'They're still with us.'

'Good,' Lexi said. 'Time for a little lane manoeuvring.'

'This is great fun, thanks everyone,' Megan said. Bella noticed that her hand was on Jack's knee. 'We can't drive forever, though. I think we need to stop at some point and Jack and I should go for a bit of a walk. Give them something to write about.'

Bella had to agree. 'You're right. This is only going to keep them interested for so long. Where should we drop you off? Jack, any ideas?'

He rubbed his chin thoughtfully, and seemed to notice the placement of Megan's hand for the first time. 'We need to be dropped off quick enough for you to then drive on, but take long enough that they see where we are and take the bait,' he said. 'How about somewhere along the cliff paths?'

Megan gave a little squeak of horror.

Bella smiled at her. 'It's okay, we won't expect you to go

anywhere dangerous, or muddy,' she added, knowing Megan didn't have the right footwear for such terrain.

'It's foggy, of course, so you can't be too far in front of them or they won't get the photos,' Rosie said.

'Everywhere's going to be foggy today,' Claire laughed. 'How about The Esplanade?'

'No, that's too open and anyone driving past can see them,' Bella said, trying to think.

'It needs to be a fairly open stretch,' Jack argued. 'How about the pier at La Rocque harbour? It's not too long, but a picturesque background for any photos with that Victorian house behind.'

'Perfect.' Bella nodded, screeching as Lexi took a sudden right and Jack, Megan and Claire fell against her, pushing her against the car door. 'Take it easy, Lexi. This isn't an episode of *Line of Duty* you know.

'I wish it was,' Lexi said. 'I really fancy that Martin Compston.'

'Can you just concentrate on your driving, please,' Aunt Rosie said. She was a fine one to criticise, Bella thought. Her driving was the most erratic of anyone she knew. Many times, she'd seen Rosie racing past the turn off to the boardwalk in her red sports car without a care in the world for anyone else.

Eventually, after several sets of road work traffic light stops, which ensured the paps' cars kept up with them, Lexi drove down Gorey hill and along the coast to La Rocque. She stopped in one of the parking spaces just before the start of the peaceful pier. 'Get out here and we'll circle back to meet you here again.'

Jack stepped out of the car, glanced briefly at Bella, and got out. 'Why don't we finish our walk along the beach and meet you at Green Island? It'll look a bit more authentic if we're actually aiming for somewhere.'

'Good idea,' Lexi said. 'If you take too long, we'll go inside the café to wait for you.'

He made a point of looking around him, pretending to check that no one was around to see them, then leaning in, took Megan's hand and helped her out.

'Good luck,' Bella and Lexi shouted, before the car moved off. 'Don't go too far in front of them, remember. We don't want you two disappearing into the fog, or all this will have been for nothing.'

Bella looked back out of the rear window as they drove off. Jack had his arm around Megan's shoulders and she had an arm around his waist. Her heart sank, seeing how perfect they looked together. Stop it, she scolded herself. He was only playing a part. He was doing it well though. Megan seemed happier than she had ever seen her before. Bella didn't blame her.

Assuming it would take the couple about twenty minutes to half an hour, depending on how slowly they walked, they continued along the coast, pulling into the car park at Green Island to wait. They sat quietly in the car for a few minutes, each lost in their own thoughts as the wind whipped up the sand on the small beach between the car park and the small island. It was mostly shrouded in fog and would be cut off from the rest of the island at the next high tide.

'Why don't we all get out and stretch our legs?' Bella suggested.

'Good idea,' laughed Claire. 'I don't know about you two, but I could do with a bit of fresh air after Lexi's driving.'

Lexi giggled. 'Cheek. If you weren't Bella's mum, I'd make you walk home.'

'What, all the way to the boardwalk?'

'Yes.'

Bella smiled and zipped up her jacket. 'Come on. Let's go

before they get back and we have to continue with our charade.' Without waiting for them to sort themselves out, she got out of the car, pulling her bobble hat down over her ears. Taking a pair of ever present gloves from her pocket, she slipped them on. She breathed in the fresh sea air and felt the tenseness in her shoulders dissipate. She could hear Lexi, Rosie and her mum chatting and laughing as they got out of the car.

'Let's go then,' Claire said, walking up to her and linking her arm through Bella's.

They walked down the slipway onto the fine, pale gold sand, the sight of which never failed to relax Bella. Hearing the other two following behind them, she squeezed her mum's arm gently and said, 'I'm loving having you back here on the island.'

'Are you?' Claire asked, seeming genuinely surprised.

'Yes, very much. I wish you'd consider staying here for good, but I know that won't happen.'

They walked on for a few paces. 'Maybe you're enjoying it so much because you know it won't last,' Claire said thoughtfully.

Bella stopped, hurt by her mother's words. 'That's a dreadful thing to say.'

'Is it?'

'Yes.' Was it, though? she thought, as they carried on walking. Maybe her mum was right. It was easier to make the most of someone if you knew there was going to be an end to it shortly. She considered her mum's words. No, she wasn't. 'You're wrong. It is wonderful getting to know you again. Properly. If you go again, then fine, I'll understand. If you ever did settle here, I really would love having you around all the time. Honestly.'

Claire pulled her to a stop and kissed her on the cheek. 'Gosh, your face is cold,' she said, placing her hand on it briefly. 'I suppose mine must be too.'

Bella laughed. 'You must be frozen after being in Sri Lanka for so long. How are you coping with this miserable weather?'

'I don't mind it at all,' Claire said, reaching down to pick up a small bit of worn driftwood. 'I thought I'd hate it, to be honest. I expected to miss Sri Lanka dreadfully, but, I don't know, maybe the time is just right for me to have come back here.'

Bella didn't want to raise her hopes, or make her mother feel pressured, but couldn't help asking, 'Would you seriously consider coming back here to stay, do you think? I mean, travelling is all you've really done since you were eighteen.'

A small Jack Russell ran past, chasing a ball. They waved at the owner who seemed to be looking for him, and Bella pointed in the direction of the little dog.

'I would,' Claire said, quietly.

Bella wasn't sure whether to take that as a definite prospect, so dropped the subject. 'It's eerie here today, but I love it. It's not often I've been down here in such thick fog.'

'I don't recall ever doing so,' her mum said.

Bella spotted two distant figures through the mist. Judging by the height and broad shoulders of the taller one, and the petite person next to him, it must be Jack and Megan.

'Do you think that's them?' she said, almost certain it was when they got closer.

'Yes.'

They stopped walking, watching in silence as Jack appeared to take Megan in his arms and kiss her. Bella gave an involuntary gasp, immediately furious with herself for doing so.

'He's only acting, remember,' her mum whispered.

'It's fine,' Bella said, forcing a smile. 'I'm just being foolish.' They began making their way to the car. 'I hope the paps got their photo.'

Her mother didn't reply for a little while, then broke the

silence by saying, 'It's fine to be upset, seeing the man you love kissing someone else.'

'It's not. There's nothing between us, and don't forget Nicki is still on the scene, whatever Jack says. Please don't tell anyone about Nicki's wedding plan.'

'You know I won't.'

'Not even Rosie,' Bella said, aware that her mother's idea of keeping a confidence was a little looser than her own. 'You know how she loves to try and make things happen between people. She's a right matchmaker, given half the chance.' She thought for a moment. 'You probably are, too.'

'A little. But I can't help it if I'm a romantic at heart.' She nudged Bella playfully. 'I won't say a word to her, or anyone else, I promise.'

Comforted by her reassurance, Bella shivered. 'They must be frozen by now. Poor Megan really feels the cold.'

'Jack probably won't even notice,' laughed her mother.

'You're right. He loves nothing better than being in the sea and that's bitterly cold most of the time.'

They reached the car to find Lexi and Rosie already sitting inside, chatting.

'You two didn't last long out there,' Bella laughed, relieved they hadn't seen her reaction to Jack and Megan on the beach. 'Did you even go for a walk?' she asked, getting inside.

'We reached the bottom of the slipway and decided that was enough for the day,' Rosie said.

'I wanted to go into the café, like we agreed, but Rosie insists we won't have enough time to order anything, much less drink it.'

'She has a point,' Bella agreed.

'She was the one who wanted to get back to the car,' Lexi giggled. 'But I didn't take much persuasion.'

They heard Jack shouting and pointing his finger at someone

behind him, before running to the car, pulling Megan along behind him.

'Hurry, get in,' he said, holding the door open for her. 'And you two, leave us the hell alone, or I'll report you.'

He got in with them. 'Better drive on, Lexi,' he said, laughing, slightly out of breath. 'I think they took that seriously enough, don't you?'

Megan giggled. Her rosy cheeks suited her. 'That was the best fun. You're an awesome kisser, Jack Collins,' she said, pouting at him.

Jack cleared his throat. 'Er, thanks.'

'Do you think they got their photos?' Rosie asked. 'Or will we have to take you somewhere else for another try.'

'Ooh, yes please,' Megan said, gazing up at Jack through her false eyelashes.

Jack smiled at Rosie, then Megan. 'I think they got all they needed. We should go back to the cottage now. Or, maybe Sacha's for a hot drink. Megan must be frozen.'

'I am a bit,' she said. 'Though I didn't notice when we were on the beach and you had your arm around my shoulders.'

'Look, there they are,' Bella said, hoping to change the subject. She pointed to the two red-faced photographers running up the beach, still taking photos of them in the car. 'Quick, Jack, pretend to shield Megan from them.'

Megan giggled. 'I'm loving this. Who knew Jersey could be so much fun.'

'Sacha's it is then,' Lexi said, putting her foot down and leaving the car park, only just missing the first hire car as it stopped to collect the photographers.

'I think they were a bit lost,' Rosie laughed. 'Good.'

They pulled out onto the road. 'I think we've given them enough to keep them busy,' Bella said, satisfied that her plan had worked. 'Let's get back to the boardwalk, and this time don't let them follow.'

'You can take your time, if you like though,' Megan said sweetly, resting her head on Jack's chest.

He gave Bella an alarmed grimace over Megan's head. 'No, I think we need to get back. I've got things to do.'

'Oh? Like what?'

'Um, I have a thing.' He frowned at Bella. 'You know, Bella. That thing we were arranging?'

Bella thought frantically of something she could use to get him out of his predicament. 'You mean planning the beach party for bonfire night?'

Jack beamed at her and her heart contracted. 'Yes, that. You remember, Aunt Rosie? I was telling you all about the silent fireworks I'd ordered, so that none of the pets get frightened on the night.'

'Ah yes, of course. Haven't you organised that yet? It's only five days away, Jack.'

'It's for the locals in the village and anyone else who wants to come,' Bella explained to Megan. 'Word of mouth is all we need. On our grapevine, that should take about ten minutes.'

'Judging by the amount of people outside the cottages this morning, I can see that you're not exaggerating,' said Megan. 'The party sounds fun.' Her voice turned sulky. 'I wish I could come along.'

'You might still be here, if this bloody fog doesn't lift before then,' Lexi said. 'I mean, I'm sure it will, but you know, if it doesn't.'

They drove in silence for a few minutes, until Megan broke it saying, 'It's Halloween, I'd forgotten. Are there any parties nearby that we could go to?'

Jack sighed. 'Not elaborate ones,' he said. 'My sister and her boyfriend are holding a get-together at the café this evening, and there'll probably be the usual kids trick or treating around the boardwalk.'

'Will you sit with me at the cottage to make sure they don't bother me?' Megan was all smiles again.

Bella only just withheld a groan. 'Lexi and I could do that. Jack will need to be at the café, as will we for some of the time, at least.'

'Yes, and Nicki will probably be after me again,' he said, almost to himself. 'She should be returning to London soon.'

Bella thought he sounded hopeful about Nicki's departure, or was that just wishful thinking? She wondered what Nicki would do when she found out about their outing today. How would she react to the photos if they did appear in the papers, showing Jack and Megan walking alone together? Her thoughts turned to the teenage kiss she'd shared with Jack at a beach party, and she wondered what it would be like to kiss him now. He had kissed her once when she was seventeen and he was nineteen after a boozy beach party, infuriating Sacha. She had made such a fuss they'd never come close to being more than friendly after that.

Lexi drove down the hill and parked round the back of the cottages. 'We can walk to the café from here,' she said. 'If we hurry, they won't see us and will think we're inside by the time they find their way back here.'

'Good plan,' Claire said, unclicking her seat belt and getting out of the car. 'Come along, hurry up.'

'You go down and I'll follow on,' Lexi said. 'I just want to check the heating's on for when Megan gets back up here.'

Bella watched the other four hurry down the hill and stayed back with Lexi. She waited for her outside the cottage, hands pushed deep into her pockets. When Lexi didn't come out, she went to find her. 'Come on, what are you doing in there?'

'I found this,' she said, holding an opened envelope in one hand, and what looked very much like a wedding invitation in the other.

Bella's heart rate soared. 'What is it?' she asked, almost wishing she hadn't.

'I know what it looks like, but it's actually an invitation to a Halloween party at the Sea Breeze.'

'But that's tonight.'

Lexi shrugged. 'I know. A bit late by way of notice. I wonder whether you've got one?'

'I doubt it.' Bella suddenly wasn't sure. It would be just like Nicki to want her to witness her wedding proposition to Jack.

'Will you go, if you do have one?'

Would she? Bella gave it a little thought. 'Yes. I would want to be there for Jack, in case she's up to mischief.'

'Good point,' Lexi said. 'Me, too.'

They left the house and hurried down the hill. The drizzle that now accompanied the fog lowered her mood even further. 'Shall I quickly pop home and see if I do have an invitation?'

'Yes, I'll come with you.'

* * *

Five minutes later they arrived at the café to find Jack and Megan sitting at a table with steaming drinks and plates of chocolate cake in front of them.

'Where have you two been?' Sacha asked. 'These two have been telling me all about your escapades this morning. It sounds great fun.'

'It was,' Bella said, assuming her mum and Rosie must have gone to visit Betty. She handed Jack the envelope she'd found lying on her doorstep. 'This is yours.'

'Ah, I wasn't sure whether to say anything, or not,' Sacha said. 'Nicki delivered one of those here for me this morning, too. She's invited me and Alessandro.'

'To what?' Jack asked, staring at the small white envelope as if it was about to burst into fire. He looked over at Bella and then back at the envelope. 'Maybe you were right to be concerned, Bella,' he said quietly.

'There's also one for you, Megan,' Lexi said. 'It was on my doorstep.'

Megan beamed at her. 'Wow, this looks fun,' she said, taking her invitation out and reading it. 'It looks like we're all invited to Nicki's surprise Halloween party. I wonder if the party is the surprise, or if it's something else?'

'I dread to think,' Sacha said, motioning for Bella and Lexi to sit down under skeleton bunting she'd strung from one corner of the café to the other. 'Your usual? Or you could try some of my strawberry fizz and Death by Chocolate cake?'

Spotting the large succulent cake on a stand on the counter, Bella nodded. She wasn't sure if she could stomach even a crumb of her favourite cake; not with the thought of what Nicki had planned for Jack that evening crashing around in her head. She could see by the looks on the other people's faces and the giggles from a group of children inspecting individual small buckets filled with sweets, that Sacha had gone to a lot of trouble to make the party fun. Bella didn't want to dampen the atmosphere by not joining in.

'I'll skip the cake, but I must try some of that,' Lexi said, pointing to two jugs of red bubbly drink.

'Are we all going to go?' Megan asked, moving the skull candle as she beamed at Bella, excited as a small child at a birthday party.

There was a brief silence until Jack said, 'Yes, I think we should.'

'I thought you were supposed to be keeping your head down,' Bella said. Then, remembering that they had only just returned from giving the paparazzi something to write about, added, 'Though I think we've already ensured your cover was blown this afternoon.'

'So, there's no reason for me to miss the party?'

Bella had to agree that there wasn't. 'Do you have something to wear?' Did she? she wondered, trying to picture everything in her meagre wardrobe.

'Yes. I brought a few new dresses with me. I might not have lived in this celeb world for long, but I know to take clothes in case the stuff stylists bring is horrible.'

'Don't the stylists put you in clothes from designers they're supposed to be promoting?'

'Mostly, maybe. Either way, I like having something of my own, just in case.'

It made sense to Bella. She wasn't sure she wanted to go to the party and didn't like to leave her mum alone at the cottage while she went out with the rest of them. Happy to have an excuse to miss it, Bella tried to sound disappointed as she said, 'I might have to do something with Mum tonight.'

'No, you're not getting out of it that easily,' Jack said. 'I heard Claire and Aunt Rosie talking earlier, when they were walking with me to the cottage, about going out for a few drinks and a catch up tonight. Aunt Rosie was saying how it's been years since they've had time for a proper chat.'

She liked to think of her mother settling back in with her old friends. Claire and Rosie had apparently been very close until her mum had fallen pregnant with Bella and gone on her travels soon after she was born.

They ate their cake and chatted a little more. Bella listened to the others' excitement about the evening building. Only Jack seemed a little subdued. She caught him looking at her and gave him what she hoped was a reassuring smile. It wasn't her fight, but he was her friend and she was going to be there to support him should he need her to and if Nicki was going to try and trap Jack into marrying her, then she wanted to be there to witness his reaction, not hear about it third-hand.

'Right,' Sacha said, collecting the empty plates and cups. 'You lot get going and give me a chance to sort things out here and figure out what I'm going to wear.'

Bella helped collect the plates and followed her into the kitchen. 'Do you really think Nicki is going to try and corner him?'

'Who knows?' Sacha said, as they stacked the large dish-washer. 'I wouldn't put anything past her.'

That was what worried Bella, too. She had been hoping Sacha could dispel some of her concerns about the evening, as she knew Nicki much better than Bella did. Never mind, she thought. She would simply have to see how things went.

'Right, I'll leave you to it. I need to try and find something suitable for tonight in my wardrobe.' She raised her eyebrows. 'It's not going to be easy.'

'Megan and I are going back to the cottages to get ready,' Lexi said, as they walked back into the café. 'Shall we all meet here and walk to the hotel together?'

'Good idea,' Bella said. 'Here, seven thirty.' She looked at her mother, chatting quietly to Rosie. 'Have a fun evening, you two. I'll catch up with you later, Mum.'

She walked back to the cottage with Jack. He barely spoke on the way and Bella wasn't sure what she could say to help him.

'You alright?' she asked quietly as she pulled off her gloves and tucked them into her coat pocket.

'Yes, fine. You don't have to worry about me.'

She smiled at him. 'That's good,' she said, only slightly comforted.

* * *

At the agreed time, they all met up at the café and walked to the nearby hotel together. Bella was relieved the party was only around the corner. She stopped by the door and leaned on a chair to adjust her shoe.

'Uncomfortable?' Sacha asked.

'Just not used to wearing heels.' Bella grimaced. 'I thought I should make an effort to at least look like I'm used to attending parties.' She didn't add that she didn't want to appear unsophisticated against Nicki's, no doubt, sleek appearance.

Jack held open the reception door to the hotel while they filed in.

'You're here for the party, I presume?' asked a smiling, handsome man in a dark grey suit.

She could hear laughter and voices coming from a nearby room. 'Yes, we are.' She read his badge and saw that he was the assistant manager and that his name was Charlie. She wondered why she hadn't seen him before and must have stared rather longer than she intended, because when she looked at his face she saw he was smiling directly at her.

'You're all local to the village?'

'Everyone except me,' Megan said, fluttering her false eyelashes at him.

Bella waited for his reaction, but supposed that he didn't

watch much television, when he nodded. 'Welcome, then. I hope this fog isn't causing you too much of a problem.'

'It was,' Megan giggled. 'But these people have been entertaining me and I have to admit that I've been having far more fun than I ever imagined.'

'That's great news.' He stepped back and indicated the double doors to the side. 'If you'd like to pass me your coats, I'll hang them up in the cloakroom. The party's through there.'

They handed him their coats and scarves and Sacha and Bella led the way, opening the doors slowly to reveal circular tables decorated with high glass vases filled with copper foliage and orange flowers. The tablecloths were pale purple, and for someone who didn't live on the island, Nicki had managed to fill the room with guests.

'Where did she find all these people?' Bella asked, scanning the faces to see if she knew any of them. She didn't seem to.

'No idea,' said Sacha.

Jack joined them, standing between the girls, an arm around each of their shoulders. 'She never did do things by halves,' he murmured. 'I recognise some of them from her firm's Christmas party last year.' He stared at one man for a few seconds. 'That's her new bloke.'

'Where?' Bella asked, intrigued. Had she read the situation wrong? It seemed so, she thought with relief.

'The smart guy over there, talking to her.'

Bella studied the man. She was sure she'd seen him somewhere before. 'Do I know him?'

'Isn't he off the telly?' Sacha asked. 'I don't think he's an actor though. Good looking enough to be one.'

Megan pushed in between Bella and Jack. 'What have I missed?'

Sacha pointed discreetly to the couple. They didn't seem very loving. He seemed determined not to make eye contact with Nicki as she leaned in close to him, talking.

'Bloody hell, he's hot!' Megan pushed forward, then reaching back, grabbed Bella's hand. 'Come along. You're supposed to be entertaining me, so introduce me to him.'

Bella snatched her hand back. 'I don't know who he is. You'll have to introduce yourself if you're determined to speak to him.'

'Fine,' she said. 'Watch me.'

As Megan strode across the room, head held high, medically enhanced boobs thrust out, Bella heard several male invitees vocalise their appreciation. She could see by the look on the younger girl's face that she was enjoying every second of their undivided attention.

'Wouldn't you just love to have that girl's confidence?' Sacha whispered to Bella.

'Ten per cent of it would do me.'

'True. Look at her go. You've got to be impressed.'

Bella was. 'Do you know, having spoken to her a bit since she got here, I've come to the conclusion that a lot of what she projects is a front. I think she's determined to be a celebrity, but doesn't have that much confidence underneath.'

Jack laughed. 'You could have fooled me.'

Alessandro arrived, and Sacha went to greet him. They returned to the others, arms around each other's waists, and Bella couldn't help thinking what a gorgeous couple they made.

'Look at Megan,' she said, and they turned to watch as Nicki spotted Megan's approach with a fixed smile on her face.

'Oh hell, I think there's going to be trouble,' Sacha said. 'Maybe it's time we found our table and sat down.'

'Good idea,' Jack agreed, crossing the room to study the table plan on a large white easel by the doorway. He indicated a table at the back of the room, by the entrance to the kitchen, and the girls followed him to find their seats.

'We're well out of harm's way here,' Bella said, relieved.

Sacha pulled a face. 'With Nicki in the room, I can't see that anywhere is really safe from her.'

'I'll get us some drinks,' Jack said, without waiting for them to argue.

Bella watched him walk over to the bar. 'He seems fairly sure that this event has nothing to do with him, doesn't he?'

Sacha nodded. 'Let's hope so. Although, to be honest, you can't force Jack to do anything he doesn't want to do.'

Good, thought Bella. She had assumed as much, but it was reassuring to hear Sacha confirm it, especially as Jack seemed to go running whenever Nicki called him. Alessandro went to join Jack at the bar.

'I wonder what your mum and my Aunt Rosie are chatting about tonight?' Sacha asked, looking amused. 'I don't know if I trust either of them to behave.'

Bella giggled. 'Me neither. They were going out for a few drinks together for a proper catch up.'

'Actually, never mind *what* they're chatting about,' Sacha said, only momentarily taking her eyes off Nicki. She shook her head and smiled at Bella. 'More like, who are they chatting *up*?'

'It doesn't bear thinking about.' Bella realised who the man standing with Nicki was. 'That's the economist, Oliver Whimsy,' she said, quietly. 'I was reading about him in a magazine at the dentist's last month. He's very good looking, don't you think?'

Sacha nodded. 'He is. You're right, too. Wow, how the hell did Nicki snap him up, he's gorgeous.'

Bella agreed, but resisted telling her friend that she didn't mind how handsome the man was, as long as he was going to keep Nicki from fighting to get Jack back.

'Who's that bloke Nicki's with?' Lexi asked, joining them at the table.

'Where've you been?' Bella asked, noticing the smile on Lexi's face.

'Never you mind.'

'Tease,' Bella smiled.

The band, which Bella hadn't noticed before, struck up a tune, and everyone began to find their tables and take their seats. Megan stopped to beam at a couple of male guests on her way back to their table. Alessandro and Jack hurried back, carrying their drinks.

'Oh heck,' Sacha groaned. 'Nicki's getting up on the stage.'

They had all sat down by the time she raised her hands and gave a little bow to the band.

'Thank you,' she said, turning back to face her captive audience. 'Welcome, dear friends, and thank you for coming to my surprise Halloween party.' She gave her guests a brilliant white smile and held her hands out. 'I've asked you here today for a celebration, but won't reveal the occasion until after you've eaten and enjoyed yourselves.'

'But we want to know now,' shouted a man Bella had seen being a little noisy at the bar when they arrived. 'Tell us, tell us, tell us,' he chanted, waving for the others to join in.

Bella and Jack exchanged unimpressed glances, as one or two of the guests half-heartedly joined in with the chants.

She had expected Nicki to be furious by the man's interruption of her speech, but instead she seemed to be considering doing as he asked, making Bella suspect that maybe the entire scene had been set up.

Nicki motioned for Oliver Whimsy to join her. 'Oliver,' she said, her voice low and enticing.

He looked, Bella thought, slightly uncomfortable but did as

Nicki asked. She took his hand and before anyone could say anything, got down on one knee in front of him. A collective gasp filled the room. 'Oliver, will you marry me?'

'Bloody hell!' bellowed one of the suited men seated at the table Oliver had just vacated. 'She's proposing.'

Bella's relief that Nicki wasn't about to ask Jack to marry her after all was soon dispelled when she saw the look of horror on the poor man's face, as he stood, statue-like, in front of her.

'Poor bastard,' Megan said. 'He looks as if he's hoping his world will implode.'

He did, Bella thought, sensing his agony. Nicki, still on one knee in front of him, clasped his left hand in hers. Bella couldn't imagine what he could possibly do next. 'This is horrible,' she said under her breath to Jack.

'You're not kidding.'

A cheer came from the table closest to Nicki. 'Well, answer her, you berk.'

It was like being a spectator sensing that a crash was about to happen. Bella wanted to look away, but couldn't.

Oliver pulled Nicki to her feet and tried to lead her away from the stage, but Bella's relief that the spectacle was about to end was short lived.

'No, Oliver darling,' Nicki said, giving a fake giggle. 'You need to give me a reply. Our audience is waiting.'

'This is horrible,' Bella murmured. 'Why would she do something like this?'

Oliver Whimsy let go of her wrist and prised her hand from his. 'Enough,' he said, loud enough for them to hear. 'I don't know why you've arranged this charade, Nicki.' He scowled at her. 'But as far as I'm concerned, we haven't known each other long enough to even contemplate getting married. I'm not sure it's something I ever intend doing.'

The guests stared silently at them, waiting to see what happened next. Bella wished she could leave but daren't draw attention to herself by moving. She noticed someone discreetly filming the entire event and couldn't imagine why they would want to record someone's humiliation in this way.

'Come on, Oliver,' Nicki said. 'Why not be brave and go for it. I have a registrar waiting to make this legal.'

'Sorry, what?' He glanced briefly towards the gawping guests and back at Nicki. 'This is insane. You do realise that, surely?'

Nicki reached up and placed her hand on his cheek. 'No, it isn't, baby. It's fun. All you have to do is say yes.' She smiled at her captive audience. 'Doesn't he, everyone?'

'She's trying to embarrass him into agreeing,' Jack said quietly. 'Poor sod.'

Oliver stared at Nicki, as if he was seeing her for the first time. 'No.'

And without saying another word, he pushed her hand away and marched out of the room.

Nicki stood for a second with her mouth open at her intended fiancé's reaction.

'Poor, silly, cow,' Megan said. 'She's got balls, I'll give her that.'

'She's arrogant and controlling, is what she is,' Sacha argued. 'That woman is always determined to get what she wants. Unfortunately for that poor guy, she wanted him.'

'He didn't look that nice, anyway,' Lexi said. 'I wonder where he went?'

The band struck up, once again, and Nicki, her face like a smiling mask, called them all onto the dance floor.

'What about the food?' Bella heard one man asking.

Bella glanced around her table, desperate to go home. 'Shall we leave?' she said. 'I don't think I can stomach any more of Nicki's ridiculous behaviour.'

Without another word, Bella, Sacha, Lexi, Megan and Jack stood up and quietly made to leave the ballroom.

'You're not staying for the meal?' Nicki said, reaching the door before them and standing in front of Jack. She seemed amused, rather than embarrassed by what had happened, and Bella had to wonder at her mental state.

'You didn't really invite us for a meal though, did you?' Jack stared at her. 'I knew you enjoyed a masquerade but this evening was a farce. Did that poor bloke even suspect you were up to something?' When she didn't react, he shook his head. 'I thought not.'

'Just be grateful it wasn't you she'd set her sights on,' Sacha said, taking his arm and leading him out.

Bella was grateful, and wondered whether this meant that Nicki and Jack were completely over. She hoped so, but knowing their history, she couldn't be sure that they wouldn't get together, yet again. Had Nicki chosen Jersey as the place to propose to Oliver simply to make Jack jealous? She wouldn't put it past her.

They congregated in the reception area. 'Where's that cute guy that took our coats?' Megan asked. 'I hope Nicki didn't scare him off, too.' The joke broke the tension in the air and they all laughed. 'That has to be the worst party I've ever been invited to,' she added.

'I'll go and find him,' Bella said, hoping they could collect their coats and leave the hotel as soon as possible. She walked through another door and down a hallway, listening out for voices. Hearing a male voice she thought might belong to Charlie, she followed the sound and reached a small ante room to find him having a cup of tea. 'Sorry, I didn't mean to disturb you.'

Blushing, he placed his cup on the small table next to him. 'No, I apologise for not being at reception. It's been a bit of a chaotic night, with one thing and the other.'

Bella sighed. 'I know Halloween is supposed to be a strange evening, but this one beats anything I've experienced before.'

'Me too,' he laughed, leading the way back to the others. 'Sorry for keeping you all waiting. I'll fetch your coats now.'

They watched him disappear into the cloakroom and waited as he kept returning until all the coats had been collected and put on.

'Thanks,' Jack said. 'I hope the rest of your evening isn't as odd.'

'So do I.'

They walked back to the boardwalk in a muted silence, which Jack eventually broke by saying, 'To make up for tonight, I think we should definitely have that bonfire on the beach some of us have been talking about.'

'Yes, good idea,' Sacha said. She looked at Megan, 'Will you still be here for it?'

'One part of me hopes not, because I need to get back to work,' said Megan. 'But the other half doesn't want to leave now I've got to know you lot better. You've shown me more fun than I've experienced in ages.'

Bella couldn't help thinking that if Megan had been a little more pleasant during their photo shoot then she would have had a much better time. She hoped that Megan's time on the island would soften her a bit and give her the confidence to believe she could survive the weird world of celebrity that she desperately wanted to remain a part of.

'We'll see you tomorrow,' Lexi said, giving Bella and Sacha a kiss on the cheek. 'Megan and I are going back to the cottages.'

'I'll accompany you both,' Jack said, pushing his hands into his coat pockets.

'We're fine, thanks,' Lexi said, smiling at him. 'I don't think the bogey man will find us between here and home.'

'Shut up, you,' Megan argued, nudging Lexi. 'If Jack wants to walk us home, then I, for one, am happy to let him do it.'

Bella stood with the others, watching as they began their short trek up the hill. Feeling raindrops on her face, she held out her hand to make sure. 'Quick, it's starting to rain,' she said, linking arms with Sacha. 'The wind has picked up.'

'Good,' she said. 'Maybe the fog will lift by the morning and Megan's team will be able to fly in for the interview and take the photos they need.'

'Time we all went home, I think.'

Lying in bed a short while later, Bella closed her eyes and listened to the wind howling around the headland on the other side of the boardwalk. Her last thought was that Jack hadn't yet returned home. She knew she shouldn't, but couldn't help imagining him finally succumbing to Megan's advances.

13

Bella was folding the top of a box of small collectibles she had just finished packing to take to a sale, when Jack raced in early the following morning. She glanced up to see that his hair was damp and so were his jeans, and he was carrying a rolled up towel, and she wondered whether he'd stayed out all night.

'You're up,' he said, his eyes wide.

She wasn't sure why he seemed so startled to see her. 'Are you okay?' she asked, concerned. 'Have you been surfing in this weather? No, forget I asked that. I can see that you have.'

'I needed to clear my head after last night.' He stared at her and took a deep breath.

Did he mean Nicki's disastrous party or what had happened after he'd reached the cottage where Megan was staying? Bella didn't dare ask.

'You shouldn't wear your jeans over a wet swimming costume,' she heard herself scold, sounding like a schoolteacher. 'You'll catch a chill.'

Jack's steps hesitated. 'I'm not.'

'But your underpants must be wet.'

'I'm not wearing any,' he said, sounding like he had a smile on his face as he continued on his way up to the bathroom to shower.

Bella carried on, choosing what pieces to pack for the antiques fayre she took part in several times each year to bolster her income. Moments later, as she was closing the next box, she sensed him watching her. She glanced at him, aware he wanted to tell her something and sat back on her heels looking up at him as he reached the bottom of the stairs. 'What is it?'

'Your mum asked me to let you know she's over at Betty's,' he said, frowning.

Bella realised she hadn't heard her mother get up. 'Already?'

'She told me to let you pack for the fayre before telling you that Betty had a fall last night.' Bella gasped. 'She's going to be fine, but your mum's going to stay with her for a few days, to look after her.'

Bella sat back on her heels. 'Sorry? What happened?'

'She went outside to call the cat in and slipped on some wet leaves near her front door.'

She stood up, wanting the full story before going to find her mother and see Betty, immediately forgetting all about the fayre. 'How do you know, and I don't?'

Jack placed a calming hand on her shoulder. 'Hey, don't panic. She's had a bit of a shock but she's going to be fine. Her wrist is broken and has a little bruising, but she's in good spirits.'

'Go on.'

'I went with her to the hospital.'

Bella couldn't understand when all this could have happened and asked him to elaborate.

'I was on my way home after a quick swim,' he shrugged. 'Hence the lack of underpants. Come to think of it, I must have left them on the beach. Damn.' He shook his head, looking annoyed at himself. 'Anyway, I was about to come inside, when I thought I heard a moan. I looked towards Betty's home, where I thought the sound had come from, and checking closer, found her lying there.'

'That's awful, poor Betty. Had she been there long?' Bella asked panicking at the thought of how cold it was last night. 'She must have been frozen.'

'I covered her with my coat and sat next to her. I didn't want to lift her in case she'd broken something that should be left, if you see what I mean.'

Bella did. 'Then what happened?'

'I called for an ambulance on my mobile and they were here in five minutes. I went with her to hospital and she had an X-ray and plaster put on her arm, and was told that she could go home, but had to take it easy, especially in view of her age.'

'Poor thing. Shouldn't she still be in hospital though?' Bella was shocked and close to tears.

'She refused to stay there. I promised the doctors I'd accompany her home and explained that we were a tight-knit community and she wouldn't be left alone. Your mum popped in just after seven and said she was happy to sit with her.'

'I'll go and see her now.'

'I thought you might want to. I'll join you,' he said, grabbing his coat.

They stepped outside and, despite the sunshine, the chill in the air took Bella's breath away.

'At least the fog has lifted for Megan,' Jack said as they walked towards Betty's home. 'She'll be able to give that interview, have her photos taken and go back to her busy life.'

Bella could picture how relieved the girl would be this morning as she looked out of the window at the sunshine. 'I suppose they'll be flying in this morning.'

'I guess so. She was saying last night that she's going to ask the magazine to take photos in Sacha's café, Jools' bookshop, your antique shop and Lexi's cottages to say thank you for keeping her entertained. If you all agree, of course.'

Bella wasn't sure whether she wanted photos to be taken of her home, but assumed that her friends would be delighted as their businesses relied more on how they looked.

'That's very thoughtful of her,' she said. 'I'm not sure about The Bee Hive though.' She tried to picture her living room plastered across one of the glossy mags. 'I change my stock so often, it's not a fixed view.'

'What?'

She smiled when she saw his confused expression and realised how odd she must sound. 'Ignore me, I'm talking nonsense. If they do want to take photos, I'd be happy to let them.'

'It makes sense. Free advertising and all that.' Jack stopped to let her walk in front as they reached Betty's house. Bella knocked lightly on the door, pushed it open and walked in to find Betty, paler than usual, sitting in her favourite armchair, her left arm in plaster and a red plaid blanket over her legs.

'Betty, are you okay?' she asked, kneeling at her elderly neighbour's feet.

'I'm fine now, pet,' she said, her voice quieter than Bella was used to hearing. 'Young Jack here found me and was a real hero.'

'I was nothing of the sort,' Jack said, his face reddening.

'Yes, you were, Jack,' Claire said, walking into the room with two cups of tea. 'Want one?'

They shook their heads.

'No, thanks,' Jack said, sitting on the arm of Claire's chair as she sat down.

'You're looking much chirpier now, Betty, I'm relieved to say,' said her mother.

She sounded concerned, and the thought of what might have happened if Jack hadn't heard Betty's groan and gone to investigate sped fleetingly through Bella's brain, causing her to shiver.

'You cold?' Betty asked. 'You can turn the heater up if you are.'

'No, I'm fine.'

Bella spotted Betty glance at her mother. She could tell they had something they were keeping from her. 'What's up?' Claire fidgeted slightly, which she always did if she was being secretive. 'Mum?'

'Your mum has agreed to move in with me for the foreseeable future, Bella,' Betty said. 'Is that alright with you? I appreciate you've only just got her back from Sri Lanka, so do say if you'd rather she didn't. I'd understand.'

Bella shook her head, trying to hide her surprise at her mother's generosity. 'No, of course she must stay with you. I'm only down the road and can pop in to see you both, any time.'

'Thanks, love,' her mum said relaxing into a smile. 'And at least this way, you can ask Alessandro to move back in and start earning rent again.'

Bella couldn't help feeling a little relieved at the thought of having her income topped up once again but felt guilty that her mother was so concerned by it. 'That's fine, Mum, really, but I was perfectly happy having you to stay with me. You do know that, don't you?'

'I do, but this way, I don't feel like a burden to you.'

'And she can look after me,' Betty added. 'Good. Now that's settled, you'd better go and break the news to Alessandro that he's got his bedroom back, so he can give in his notice at the hotel.'

'If you're certain?' Bella asked, to be doubly sure they were happy with the move.

'Yes,' her mum insisted. 'It suits us all very well. Now, go and tell him before he ends up paying for another night at that place.'

She kissed them both and leaving Jack behind to chat, ran to the Sea Breeze Hotel to try and find Alessandro.

The first person she met was Charlie, the assistant manager from the night before. 'You're not still on duty, surely?' she asked.

'About to clock off, thankfully.'

She asked if he knew where she'd find Alessandro Salvatore.

Charlie pointed to the restaurant. 'I believe he might still be in there. He's got company though.' He lowered his voice. 'By the look on his face when I last saw him, he'll more than likely be glad of your interruption.'

'Nicki?' Bella asked, wondering how she had persuaded Alessandro to eat at the restaurant when he could have gone to Sacha's café for breakfast instead.

Charlie nodded. 'Yes.'

'Poor man.'

'I agree. Right, time for me to get going. Bye.'

Bella gave him a wave and then bracing herself, went to the restaurant to find Alessandro sitting at a table opposite Nicki, with drinks in front of them. His eyes had a far-away look to them and he seemed to be nodding every so often. She couldn't help feeling sorry for him. She waited until he'd taken a mouthful of coffee while Nicki ranted, then inserted herself between them and rested a hand on his shoulder.

'Good morning,' Bella said. 'Sorry to interrupt.' She wasn't sorry at all, and Nicki clearly sensed it.

'We're actually in the middle of an important conversation,' she snapped, glaring at Bella.

'It seemed a little one-sided from where I was standing,' Bella said, a fixed smile on her face. 'I'm afraid I need to have a private word with Alessandro. It's important and it won't wait. Sorry.'

Nicki stared at her. Bella could tell she didn't want to leave them, but had no reason to stay. 'I've said all I need to, anyway,' she grumbled, before standing and marching off.

'Thank you,' Alessandro said, putting down his cup and motioning for Bella to take a seat. 'That lady, she is very strange.'

Bella nodded, amused. 'Does that mean you'll be happy not to stay here and risk eating your breakfast with guests like her?'

'I do not understand.'

Bella lowered her voice. 'Would you like to return to your old room at my cottage?'

His eyes lit up and he beamed at her, giving her the answer she knew he would. 'Very much, Bella. But what about your mama?'

'Finish your breakfast and sort out your bill and pack your things. I'll see you back at the cottage when you're ready. I'll tell you everything then.'

* * *

'Is very good to be back here,' Alessandro said ten minutes later, unpacking his clothes as Bella changed the bedding in his room. 'It is a good hotel but some of the people staying, like Nicki, they are strange.'

Bella laughed. 'Hopefully she'll be gone soon,' she said. 'There's trouble whenever she's around, or so it seems.'

'Jack, he must be happy she is going?'

Bella agreed. 'After last night's dramas, I should think we'll all be looking forward to a rest from her and her antics.' She hung his bath towel on the hook on the back of the bedroom door, wondering afresh why Nicki had really returned to the island, if it wasn't to win Jack back. 'Do you think you and Sacha will move in together at some point?' She knew it was nosy to ask but hoped he wasn't planning on moving out too soon.

He shrugged. 'I am uncertain. We have only known each other a few months and I think it is romantic to stay at her flat only some nights.'

She had to agree. It was. Bella wondered what would happen if she and Jack ever did get it together. They already lived in the same house but it would be odd to move into the same room with Alessandro living here, she mused. Then, reminding herself that they hadn't so much as been on a date, let alone started a relationship, she smiled.

'You are amused?'

She realised Alessandro had finished unpacking and was probably wondering what she was doing. 'Sorry, I was just thinking about something my mum said,' she fibbed.

Alessandro closed the small wardrobe doors. 'I must go and work now. I need to check on the Isola Bella. We are closing down for the winter and need for it all to be cleaned.'

It was sad to think of the boardwalk being so quiet after the busy summer season. The days had passed too quickly.

'Jack, he was telling me he has seen more of those strange symbols on the beach yesterday,' Alessandro said as they made their way downstairs.

'I didn't know.' She was surprised he hadn't mentioned anything to her. 'Is that the only one you've seen lately?'

'Yes, apart from the one on the bookshop windowsill two weeks ago,' he said. 'Still, no one knows who does this?'

'No. No idea. Although,' she smiled, 'knowing the locals, I'm surprised no one's sussed who it is yet, or what they mean, but I must admit, I quite like the mystery element.'

They walked down stairs. 'Will you be coming to the bonfire party that Jack's arranging?' Bella asked.

He nodded. 'Sacha, she says she is making the toffee apples.' He pulled a confused face. 'I have never had these before, but I am interested to discover how they will taste. I am to help her make them.'

Bella laughed. 'I like the toffee bit better than the apple. But then I've always had a sweet tooth.' She noticed the time on her deco wall clock and gasped. 'Bugger, I was supposed to go to the cottage and check up on Megan and Lexi. With any luck they'll be able to do the photo shoot and interview today and she can go home.'

'She is a funny girl. Very nice, I think.'

'She is much nicer than I thought at first,' Bella admitted, grabbing her coat. 'Lock up when you go out, will you?'

* * *

She arrived at Megan's cottage out of puff and red in the face after running up the hill. She really needed to get more exercise, she decided, and instantly changed her mind. Sport was not for her, unless it was swimming in the sea in front of her cottage.

She knocked on the door, hearing loud voices inside. She couldn't make out if they were angry or simply excited.

'Hi,' Megan shouted as she pulled open the door and stepped back to let her in. 'Isn't it a gorgeous day? I couldn't believe how beautiful this place looks in the sunshine. We're going to go down to the boardwalk as soon as Abel decides his plan for the first photos.'

She finally took a breath and Bella nodded. 'Sounds fun,' she said, looking forward to seeing how the shoot turned out. 'I'm so glad the fog lifted and the crew got here safely.'

'Me too. I was beginning to worry, as you know.' She leaned her head closer to Bella, glancing in the direction of the kitchen area where the others were congregated. 'Did you see the paper?' Megan asked quietly, pushing a copy to Bella. 'Abel was furious, so was my agent, until I insisted I knew nothing about them being taken. They were scared it might cause problems for my exclusive feature with the magazine but I promised them I didn't speak to the paps and that the photos were taken without my knowledge.' She giggled. 'My agent has been fielding phone calls for the last hour from other papers wanting interviews with me, so our plan worked.'

'Good, I'm pleased,' she said. Turning her attention to the article on the front page, she read, 'Who's the mystery hunk with celeb queen, Megan Knight?' Bella gazed at the blurry photos of Jack with his arm around Megan's shoulders looking as if he was bending to kiss her. Their body language certainly gave the impression they were a couple in love. 'You can see that it's you two, sort of. Thankfully the fog is so thick they appear to have been taken slyly. Has Jack seen them?'

'I told him about them and he looked them up on his phone. He seemed pleased that they weren't very clear.'

Bella could imagine Jack being happy for his identity to remain unknown.

'I'm still hoping I can stay here for Jack's bonfire party,' Megan said, folding the paper and placing it on the window sill. 'I'd hate to miss out and it sounds as if it's going to be fun. After all,' she said, barely taking a breath, 'I've never spent bonfire night on a beach.'

Bella hadn't considered how unusual Jack's idea was until now. 'Me neither.'

She followed Megan in to join the others. Abel stopped

speaking as soon as he spotted them, nudging the woman next to him, who instantly looked up.

'Hey, Bella,' Abel said, beaming as he pushed back the sleeves of his black woolly jumper to reveal his muscular forearms. 'Great to see you again.' He left the others and came over. 'Megan, they're ready to finish your make-up and then you can change. We'll get on with the first batch of photos.'

He led Bella outside. She breathed in the fresh autumn air, the scent of a bonfire from a nearby garden mixing with the salty sea air.

'Sorry to drag you out,' he said quietly. 'Firstly, I wanted to thank you for helping us find somewhere for Megan to stay.' He looked around him, smiling. 'This really is an incredibly beautiful area. You live nearby, I understand.'

'I have a cottage down there.' She pointed down the hill in the direction of the boardwalk. 'Just by the sea. It is lovely.'

'I can see now why you wouldn't want to live in London.'

Bella loved the city, but only for short periods of time. 'I think when you're an island girl, like I am, then you always want to return. I lived in Kingston upon Thames for a few years when I was at uni and I loved it. Now, though, I'm happy to be back here.' She couldn't help wondering why he had brought her away from the others. 'Was there something you wanted to discuss with me?' she asked, hoping he might have a hand-modelling assignment she could do.

'Yes.' He began walking along the pathway in front of the house. 'A couple of things.'

'Go on,' she said, intrigued.

'Did you hear about the photos those paps took?'

'Yes, she's just shown them to me.'

Abel took a deep breath. 'Look, I don't want to cause any friction between her and your friends,' he said. 'But do you think there's anything between her and your friend, Jack?'

Bella shook her head. 'No, why?'

Abel led her further away from the cottage and lowered his voice. 'She's just making a name for herself and if my girlfriend thought Megan was getting too attached to him, she might be concerned.'

'Because Jack lives here?' Bella asked, unsure what was troubling Abel.

'Because she'd rather Megan focus on her budding career than a new relationship.'

Bella could see he was finding their conversation a bit difficult, so nodded. 'I think it was probably a very short-lived thing between them,' she said, hoping Abel believed her.

'Good. That's a relief. Megan mentioned that you and your friends have worked hard to make her stay here fun,' he said, changing the subject. 'She was hoping to pay you back a bit by using your businesses as a backdrop for the magazine shoot. She's being so amenable at the moment, which I'm sure you recall from your work with her, is unusual. This shoot is important. It's worth a lot of money to my partner, and to me, and we're keen to keep her happy and get the job done before she remembers how she usually behaves.'

Bella couldn't help smiling. 'Would we be paid?' she asked, aware she was probably being cheeky. She was sure that Jools and Sacha would be happy enough for their bookshop and café to be included in the glossy magazine, as would she with The Bee Hive. That alone would be enough to draw in new customers.

He stopped walking and moved his weight from one foot to the other. 'I'm sure something can be arranged. So, what do you think they'll say?'

'Will you be including, Isola Bella, the *gelateria*, too?'

'If the owner was one of the people looking after Megan, then yes.'

'Great. I'll tell Alessandro. He was going to close the place down today for the winter. I'm sure he'd rather have stock and furniture in there for the photos.'

'I should think he would.'

'I'll go and ask them all now, while you get on.' She couldn't wait. 'I guess you've already had the ok from Lexi?'

'Yes,' he said, indicating the middle cottage. 'Although, she's insistent that we are careful not to disturb the tenant in the other one.'

Bella hadn't realised Lexi had let the third cottage and frowned. 'I thought she was keeping it empty?'

'That was the plan,' he said, his voice barely above a whisper. 'But she insists he won't be bothering Megan and won't be staying very long.'

'Fine,' she said, hoping Lexi was right. 'I'll be back as soon as I can. Oh, and Abel?'

'Yes, Bella,' he said, seeming relieved at how their conversation had turned out.

'It's a yes from me. I'd be delighted for you to take photos in and around my cottage. The Bee Hive, you can't miss it.'

His eyebrows knitted together. 'The what?'

She wished she hadn't said anything. 'Just look for the blue cottage, it's the only one on the boardwalk.'

She hurried down the hill to find Sacha. This really was great news. Who could have predicted that this unexpected boost in income would come from Megan, of all people? She really must be careful not to make assumptions about people before getting to know them properly first.

She reached the boardwalk and ran to Alessandro's *gelateria*, finding it locked up. 'Bugger, where is he?' she moaned, retracing her steps and then hurrying to the café, almost bumping into him as she went in. 'There you are,' she said, breathlessly telling him all that Abel Reed had said to her. 'So, if you're interested, set up your place quickly so that it looks its best.'

'Thank you,' he said, beaming at her. 'I will go and find Fin to help me.'

Sacha came over from behind the counter and kissed him before he left. She gave Bella a suspicious look. 'What are you up to?'

'You'll never guess what we'll all be doing today.'

She quickly repeated all that she'd told Alessandro and then turned to leave. 'I have to find Jools and then go and give my place a quick dust and run the hoover around.'

'Can't you ask Claire to help?'

With all the excitement, Bella hadn't realised that Sacha didn't know about Betty's fall. She explained what had happened and that her mum had agreed to move in to care for Betty. 'Which is why Alessandro has moved back to my cottage,' she finished.

'So that's what he came to tell me,' Sacha said guiltily. 'I kept putting him off because I was busy in here, and then you arrived and off he went.' She smiled at Bella. 'I'm so pleased he's back at your place. He was so happy there.'

'You don't think you'll be moving in together any time soon?' Bella asked nervously, hoping her friend didn't think she was being too nosy.

'Not just yet,' Sacha said, glancing out of the window at some noisy seagulls. 'I'm enjoying this old-fashioned courting period. I've never really had a relationship like this one before and want this stage to last for a while before moving on to the next phase.'

Bella could understand completely. 'Good for you,' she said, giving her friend a tight hug. 'Right, I'd better be off.' She pulled open the door. 'You haven't seen Jack anywhere, have you?'

Sacha pointed out to the calm sea. 'He's gone out with Tony the fisherman. It's his first day working for him.'

Bella felt a twist in her gut and wished again that Jack hadn't taken the job. She hadn't even wished him good luck earlier – had forgotten all about it. She had lived on the boardwalk long enough to know how quickly the sea could change from being calm and gentle to wild if a storm blew in from one of the other Channel Islands or over from France.

'Don't look so concerned,' Sacha said. 'Tony is very experienced. Jack will be happy as ever out at sea all day. I'll only be concerned if he ever ends up back in an office job. He hates sitting at a desk and having to wear a suit all day.'

She was right. And anyway, Bella thought, it really wasn't wise to show such concern for someone who was supposed to be just a friend. 'I know,' she said. 'I can't imagine how he coped working in the city. He must have felt like a caged animal.'

'Probably behaved like one too, on occasion,' Sacha laughed. A couple entered the café. 'Right, we'd better get on. Tell Mr Reed I'm more than happy for my café to be featured in his shoot and say thank you to Megan for suggesting it. Whether he pays me or not,' she lowered her voice. 'But don't tell him that bit, obviously.'

Laughing, she walked off and showed the couple to a table.

Bella left, staring out to sea, willing Jack to come home safely, before arriving at the bookshop to see Jools, the familiar brass bell jangling its welcome as she pushed open the door.

'Good morning,' Jools' grandmother called from her seat behind the worn wooden counter. Looking up and seeing Bella, her smile widened. 'How are you, young lady?' she said, fondly. 'Jools and I were talking about the new symbol that's appeared on the boardwalk. Have you seen it?' Bella nodded. 'I also hear from Jools that you've got an unexpected visitor.'

Bella nodded. Her nan and Jools' grandmother had been school friends and she occasionally kept in touch with her mum. 'It's been fun having Mum around, Mrs Jones. She's moving in with Betty, after her fall this morning.'

'I heard about that. Poor Betty.'

Bella heard clattering coming from the small kitchen behind the shop. 'Morning, Jools!' she shouted.

'I'll be with you in a sec!' Jools called, appearing moments later carrying one mug and a cup and saucer. 'Sorry, Gran needs her tea.' She grinned at her grandmother and placed their drinks on the counter. 'So, you've had a lot going on, haven't you?'

Bella smiled at her pink-haired friend. 'It has been a little busier than usual, yes. That's partly why I'm here.'

Jools and her grandmother stared, waiting for her to continue. 'Go on,' said Jools. 'I can tell it's exciting. Is it something to do with the drama at that party last night?'

'No,' she said, aware she was dragging the intrigue out as far as she dared.

'Bella, what?'

She explained about Megan's magazine deal and that she had asked that they include the bookshop in the photos.

She watched as her friend and her grandmother exchanged glances without speaking.

'We would be very happy for them to come and take their photos,' her grandmother said. 'But we'll need to clean the place first.'

Jools didn't look very happy at this suggestion. 'I think the dustiness gives this place character.'

Bella looked around. It wasn't dusty at all, but she knew Jools' grandmother was very particular about the cleanliness of her beloved shop.

'I'd better go,' Bella said. 'I said I'd report back as soon as I'd spoken to everyone, so that they can plan their day.'

'Will they be here this morning, do you know?' Mrs Jones asked.

'No idea. It might even be tomorrow. Is that okay?'

'Will they be paying us anything?' Jools asked.

Bella was aware that it was harder for Jools and her grandmother to make a living than she and Sacha. People loved to visit their shop but they didn't make much money and Jools was always trying to sell her beautiful paintings to top up their income. 'Yes, but I'm not sure exactly how much.' She turned to leave, stopping at the shop doorway. 'I forgot to mention, I found some second-hand books in a lot I bought at an auction,' she said and after promising to deliver them later, rushed back to find Abel and tell him that everyone was happy for their homes and businesses to be included in the shoot.

Bella left to return to the boardwalk and was distracted by a movement in the furthest cottage from Lexi's. She hesitated, just as the door opened and a disgruntled looking Oliver Whimsy walked out. He nodded an acknowledgement in her direction. Stunned to see him there, she smiled and waited for him to get into the waiting taxi and leave.

So that was Lexi's new tenant. She couldn't help wondering what had happened since the party between him and Nicki. Probably nothing, judging by the speed he'd left.

She arrived back at the boardwalk out of puff and decided that she really needed to get fitter, after all. The traipsing up and down the hill between her home and the cottages had been exhausting, but she needed to get home and check everything was in its place. The photo shoot was an opportunity she didn't want to miss.

* * *

Two hours later, Bella stood back, her gloved hands on her hips as she surveyed her freshly polished and vacuumed living room. As a small business, it worked well enough, but if they did get paid a fee, however small, for the images from Abel, it would give her a little breathing space.

Spotting a candelabra that needed moving slightly to the left, Bella stepped forward to move it and was distracted by cheers outside the cottage. Something was going on, but she couldn't imagine what at this time of year.

She pulled on her jacket and went outside to investigate. A crowd of people, mainly women, were leaning against the railings and whooping in delight at something going on down on the beach.

'Excuse me,' she said, gently manoeuvring past two of them to get a good look at what was causing all the excitement. Bella saw cameras, and a young guy holding a large white screen with a spotlight trained on it. Megan, looking stunning in a pretty yellow sundress, was waving to someone in the sea.

Craning her neck, Bella tried to see past a woman with wild curly hair in front of her. 'Jack?' she gasped, spotting him striding out of the water, surfboard under one arm as he raked the fingers of his other hand through his wet, sun-kissed hair.

'By all the saints,' said an elderly woman next to her. 'If that isn't an angel in human form coming out of the sea down there.'

Bella's stomach gave a little flip. She had to agree. 'He is pretty amazing, isn't he?' she said aloud without meaning to.

'He is H-O-T,' said another. 'Just give me five minutes with that man.'

'Hey,' Bella said, disliking the tone. 'He's my friend, thank you very much. Not a piece of meat. You wouldn't like it if a crowd of men were yelling like this over a female.'

'Whatever,' the woman replied, looking slightly red in the face.

'Oh, come on,' said a young woman whose face she couldn't see. 'Don't tell me you wouldn't pounce on him, given half a chance.'

Indignant to be thought of in such a way, Bella glared in the direction of the unknown voice. 'I most certainly would not,' she insisted, thinking how rude some people could be.

'Hey, look at her with her flowery pink gloves on,' the woman sneered. 'What's the matter? Couldn't you lower yourself to wear woollen ones like the rest of us?'

'I've been cleaning, if you must know,' she argued, not wishing to share her real reason. Telling this woman that she was a hand-model and had to protect her skin for photo shoots would only cause further mockery and she wasn't in the mood for an unnecessary argument. Plus, she was too pleased to see Jack back safely to be really angry.

Realising she was missing the scene on the beach, she made her way to the railings to get a better look at what Jack was doing. She had seen him on the beach many times before, but had never seen him look more gorgeous than he did right now.

He had been sent back into the sea, so the photographer could retake the photos. She had thought he was meant to be working with Tony at sea all day, so Bella couldn't understand why he was here at all. She watched as he immersed himself into the water before standing once more, droplets of sea falling from his muscular arms as they pushed his hair back from his forehead. She couldn't imagine them ever being able to take more perfect photos of any man.

Then, she noticed Abel with his hand up as he spoke to the photographer. She watched as he moved around and while Jack re-enacted his walking out of the sea, the photographer took a photo of Megan from the other side, including the watching crowd.

Despite Megan being the celebrity, it seemed like Jack was the star of the show. Looking at him more closely, as he emerged from the sea, she detected him shivering slightly.

'We're done here,' Abel shouted. He waved at the uninvited audience. 'Thanks for coming, ladies and gents. Much appreciated. If you buy the magazine next week you might see yourselves in one of the photos.'

Bella pushed her way out of the group and returned to her cottage to fetch a towel for Jack. He must be frozen out there, she mused. It was November, after all, and despite the bright sunshine, it was colder than usual.

She returned to the boardwalk and ran down the steps to the beach. Spotting her, Jack waved and began running over, surfboard still under his arm. She saw Abel, Megan and the rest of the crew following slowly as she rushed over to him.

He beamed at her. 'Is that towel for me?'

'Well, it isn't for me,' she laughed, opening it as he dropped his surfboard onto the soft golden sand and handing it to him. 'I thought you were out with Tony on his boat all day.'

'He managed to catch his quota of fish early, so we came back and I was roped into this shoot.' He wrapped it around his shoulders. 'Bloody hell, it's freezing out here. Come on, let's get back to the cottage.' He picked up his surfboard and noticing several of the women from the crowd coming towards them, lowered his voice. 'Did you hear that lot earlier?' he asked, waiting for Bella to go in front of him up the granite stairs.

'Yes,' she said. 'Here they come. I think you have a bit of a fan club forming.'

'Hurry into the cottage then,' he laughed. 'Move it. Quickly.'

She opened the door and they raced inside, slamming it shut and locking it behind them. Turning the shop sign from Open to Closed, Bella followed Jack through the kitchen to the courtyard outside, where he put down his surfboard. He'd dropped his towel and she had to concentrate on not letting her eyes stare at his bottom in wet, navy swimming shorts.

Jack picked up his towel from the floor and turned to say something to her when she wasn't expecting it, catching her gazing at him.

He frowned very lightly, almost so that she wasn't sure his expression had altered at all.

She cleared her throat. 'That was close,' she said, her voice tight. Relief flooded through her as someone rapped the brass knocker heavily against the front door. 'I bet you never thought today was going to work out like this?'

'No,' he said thoughtfully.

Transfixed by his gaze, she couldn't seem to make her eyes look away from his deep blue ones.

'Bella,' he said quietly, stepping forward. 'I want to talk to you about something.'

They locked eyes.

'Oi, you in there!' bellowed a woman outside. 'I thought this place was open today. It usually is.' The doorknocker rapped once again. 'Hey!'

Bella glanced over her shoulder at the door. 'Maybe I should open up and see if they want to buy something?' she said, assuming he wanted to discuss the bonfire party. 'Can it wait?'

'No.' Without taking his eyes away from hers, he lowered his head to kiss her. Unable to resist, Bella melted into his kiss. She had always mocked films where people heard choirs and angels singing, but when his lips touched hers, she wasn't sure if she didn't hear exactly that.

The woman at the door shouted again, her voice suddenly reminding Bella of Sacha. She leapt back from Jack as if his lips had stung hers.

'What's the matter?' he asked, a hurt look in his eyes. 'Haven't I read you right? Don't you have feelings for me?'

'No, it's not that,' she said, shaking her head, hating having to stop what had been so magical between them. She was scared to open up to him in case it wasn't real. 'I can't do this.' Her eyes filled with tears. 'You know what happened last time.'

'Things are different now,' he argued.

'Are they though?' She shook her head again. 'I can't, Jack, I'm sorry.'

14

Bella was walking hand in hand with Jack along the boardwalk, autumn leaves crunching underfoot. She was perfectly capable of walking without holding his hand but Jack had insisted it was more slippery than usual with all the wet leaves on the ground. 'And what if you do fall and break your fingernails?' he said, which scared her.

'Bella!'

Someone was calling her name from far away. Concentrating on working out who it was, she woke with a fright. 'A dream,' she said miserably.

She stared at her bedside clock trying to get her sleepy eyes to focus. She'd barely seen Jack during the past four days. But today was Guy Fawkes Day and they wouldn't be able to avoid each other with the bonfire party on the beach to prepare for.

Megan would be back too, she remembered. Lying back down, Bella mused how much she now liked the scatty, flirtatious girl.

Jack. She couldn't help wondering if he had left for the day, or whether he was lying asleep on the other side of the wall. One wall was all that separated them. How far would their kiss have gone if she'd let it? He hadn't mentioned it since and neither had she.

She had spent the time focusing on her business and Jack had left early, most days, to go fishing with Tony. She couldn't help wondering how he would have avoided her if his work hadn't provided him with a reason to be out before she got up but assumed he probably would have gone surfing instead.

Bella was relieved her mother was staying with Betty because Claire would have sensed the tension in the cottage and want to sort it out. Bella wasn't ready for that and didn't think Jack was either.

No point lying here wallowing, she thought, unable to stay in bed a moment longer. She pulled open her curtains. It was barely dawn but she noticed someone crouching down near to the sea wall opposite her cottage. She peered down to try and see what the person was doing. It was a man wearing a dark hoodie. His hand moved back to reach for something to reveal a symbol built of pebbles. She covered her mouth with her hand to stifle a gasp, desperate not to alert him to her presence.

Moving slowly back from the window, she quickly dressed in her jeans and a jumper and went outside, unable to resist uncovering who had been behind the mysterious symbols appearing over the past few months. Thankfully, the sound of her footsteps were masked by the noise of the waves breaking on the beach. Bella barely breathed as she crept up next to the man.

'Tony?' She couldn't believe it. Why would he be doing something like this?

He stood up, mouth open, seemingly lost for words. 'Bella, I…'

She hated to think that she had given him a shock. And now that she was standing in front of him, wished she had left him alone. It wasn't as if his symbols were hurting anyone. 'Are you okay?'

He stared at her and then down at the partially formed symbol. 'You must wonder why I've been doing this?'

'We've all been curious about them,' she admitted. 'Do you want to carry on? I won't tell anyone it was you.'

At that moment, her mother stepped out of Betty's cottage and, seeing them, walked over to join them. 'What are you two doing out here so early? Is anything the matter?'

Bella cringed. She didn't like to share Tony's secret. She exchanged glances with him.

'It's me,' he said quietly. 'I've been the one leaving the symbols. You probably think I'm a little odd.'

Claire frowned. She reached out and placed a hand on his right shoulder. 'I heard your wife died a year or so ago,' she said. 'Are these for her?'

Bella didn't dare speak, but watched as Tony nodded. 'She had a tattoo of this symbol on her wrist. She designed it herself and said that it represented our family. When I have a difficult day coping without her, I come out here when no one's around and leave a symbol as a message to her.' He gave Bella a sideways glance. 'I know she won't see it, but it helps somehow.'

'Are your children at home?' Claire asked, pointing at his cottage a few doors down from Betty's.

He shook his head. 'They're staying with my wife's parents for a few days.'

'Then why don't you come with me to Betty's? She still asleep, but you know you can always confide in her, and I'd like to think you could trust me too. I find it helps to talk to someone.'

Bella watched him consider her mum's invitation, hoping he would accept. 'There's no harm in sharing how you feel,' she said.

'It's so long since I spoke to anyone about her,' he said, almost to himself. After a moment's hesitation, he nodded. 'Yes, if you're sure you have the time,' he said, staring at Claire. 'I think I'd like that.'

'Good,' she said, smiling. 'Let's go.'

He looked at Bella. 'Don't look so worried. I'm glad you caught me. Will you put those pebbles back on the beach, so no one sees them?'

She nodded and watched her mother and Tony go to Betty's cottage, thinking how everyone was fighting their own battle.

She tidied away the pebbles, trying to make sense of how lonely Tony must have been yet none of them had noticed because he had kept himself to himself and either worked or focused on his small children.

She remembered Megan was arriving mid-morning and that she had promised to take her for a walk along the beach. She was still surprised by the girl's fondness for the place but secretly thrilled about it too. Returning to her cottage, she showered and dressed, then made her way to the bookshop to see Jools. The bell jangled to announce her arrival and she saw Mrs Jones seated at the counter, crocheting.

'Good morning, young Bella. How are you today?' She dropped a gravy bone treat for Teddy onto the floor. The little Jack Russell was popular with customers but had a tendency to run outside if the door was left open. 'Quit your begging, or you'll not have your walk on the beach.' Mrs Jones looked up at Bella. 'Jools has gone off to take photos of someone's garden she's been commissioned to paint,' she said. 'I've no idea when she'll be back and this one is driving me nuts, whining.'

'Would you like me to take him for a walk?'

'No, lovey, you've got more than enough to be getting on with.' She placed her crocheting onto the counter. 'Now, tell me how your mum and Betty are getting along. I know your mother's a free spirit, but I think the two of them will be fine living together.'

Bella had thought so too but it was a relief to hear Mrs Jones say so. 'I agree. At least I hope it works out. I want Mum to be happy, but I know she's used to her independence and living with me might have made her miss that a little.'

'Do you think she'll stay put now she's back?' Mrs Jones asked.

Bella shrugged. 'I'd like to think so. For the first time since she's been back, I can imagine it. I've never felt that before.'

Mrs Jones nodded sagely. 'Well, it's about time she settled down. It's taken her long enough.'

Bella knew Mrs Jones was fond of her mother and wasn't being mean, but still felt the need to defend her. 'Some of us are freer spirits than others,' she said.

'Yes, lovey, and some are given responsibilities earlier than they should have them.'

Bella knew she was referring to the couple of years she'd cared for her grandmother when she was unable to do much for herself. 'I was happy to be here with Nan, Mrs Jones. Mum would have felt trapped. It worked out for the best.'

'Maybe so.' Mrs Jones reached out and patted Bella's left hand. Teddy barked, just once. 'That's him telling me he wants to go out,' she said, sighing heavily. 'If you want to fetch his lead from the back of the kitchen door. If you really wouldn't mind, I'd appreciate you taking him for a walk.'

'I'd love to,' she said, keen to help.

'His ball is there too. Just be careful not to throw it up onto the rocks. It doesn't matter how high it's thrown up there, the little devil will charge up to fetch it. He got stuck twice before and the second time damaged one of his front legs.'

'Don't worry, Mrs Jones,' Bella reassured her. 'I'll be careful not to do that.' She attached Teddy's lead, said goodbye to Mrs Jones, and left the shop.

'So, shall we give Lexi a call and see if Megan has arrived yet?' She took her mobile phone from her jacket pocket and located Lexi's number. 'Hi Lexi, how are you? Have you got any idea when Megan's expected to arrive? I promised to take her for a walk on the beach and I've Mrs Jones' dog, Teddy, with me. I thought I'd walk them both at the same time.'

'She's just arrived actually,' said Lexi. 'I'll put her on.'

'Hi Bella,' Megan said, sounding very excited. 'I'm so buzzing to be back here. I was determined to be at Jack's party tonight, although my agent wasn't very happy and we had a bit of a row. But I told her that I'm busy at the moment and I need a break. Being here over Halloween showed me that I really did need to take time out.'

'Good, I'm glad,' Bella said, thrilled to hear how happy Megan sounded. 'I've got Teddy here, he's a little Jack Russell and he's desperate for walk on the beach. How about I collect you now and we go together?'

'I'd love to, but no need to come and get me. I'll walk down to you. I'm sure I won't get lost. See you in ten minutes?'

Bella laughed. 'That's great, I look forward to seeing you.' She ended the call, thinking how different Megan seemed now that she'd got to know her. If only she had been nicer in the first place, they could have been friends before now. Better late than never, Bella thought.

She decided to pop to the café while she waited for Megan to arrive. 'Shall we go and see Sacha?' she asked.

As if Teddy understood he gave a quick little bark and frantically wagged his tail. Bella wondered if maybe it was time she got her own dog. She loved dogs. She especially wanted one of the rescue dogs that had been brought to the island that she'd seen on online. She'd spotted one on the website. He wasn't very cute and no one seemed to want him. Maybe she should make some enquiries.

She peered through the glass of the café door. As it was quiet, she decided that Sacha wouldn't mind her taking Teddy inside. She opened the door and waved at her friend.

'How lovely to see you,' Sacha said, bending down to stroke Teddy 'I've got something for you, little man. Let me go and get it for you.'

She disappeared into the kitchen and came back with some chopped up chicken, which she put on the floor in front of the little dog, and they watched while he wolfed it down.

'I hope Mrs Jones doesn't mind him being fed,' Bella said. 'I don't want to annoy her the first time I take him out for a walk. It wouldn't be the best thing to do, would it?'

'She won't mind,' Sacha said. 'In fact, whenever she comes in here with Jools I give him a little bowl of chicken. He expects it now.'

Bella laughed. 'I can't say I blame him.' Something caught her eye. It was Megan, walking around on the boardwalk, looking for her. 'I better go. I promised Megan I'd take her for a walk on the beach. I thought it would be more fun with Teddy.'

She gave Sacha a brief hug, and checking that Teddy had finished his chicken, patted him on the head. 'Come on, Teddy, let's go.'

She left the café and waved at Megan, who looked much more relaxed than the last time she'd seen her. 'Lovely to see you,' she said. 'Shall we go straight down?'

Megan nodded and followed Bella and Teddy down the granite steps onto the soft sand where Bella unclipped the dog's lead. She took his tennis ball out of her pocket and threw it for him to chase. He raced off after the ball, going so fast that he missed it. Turning around, he retraced his steps and grabbed it, bringing it back to be thrown once again.

'What a cute little dog,' Megan said.

Bella noted that she didn't actually touch the dog and smiled to herself. 'He is. How have you been?' asked Bella.

'Fine, thanks.' Megan pointed in Teddy's direction and smiled. 'I think we need to throw his ball for him again.'

Bella reached it first, picked it up and threw it away from the rocks. Next it was Megan's turn. She picked up the ball and threw it back the other way.

'We have to be careful,' Bella said, thinking of Mrs Jones. She had no intention of having to break the news to the old lady that her dog was stuck up the cliffs. 'The owner is most insistent that we don't throw the ball onto the rocks because apparently, Teddy has no sense when it comes to chasing after it. She said he's already been stuck up there twice and once I gather, he hurt himself.'

Megan picked up the ball and hurled it. For someone so slight, Megan threw with a huge amount of strength. 'Oh, no!' she shouted, covering her mouth with her hand.

Bella looked over to see what was wrong, horrified to see the ball had bounced halfway up the rock face. 'Quick! Grab Teddy.'

He'd scooted out of Megan's hands before she could get hold of him and was running after his ball.

'Teddy!' Bella screamed, but the little dog completely ignored her and ran flat-out towards the rocks.

'Surely he's not going to run up there,' said Megan, looking dismayed. 'Aw hell, I think he is.'

'We're going to have to get him,' Bella said, chasing after him, trying not to panic. 'Otherwise he's going to get stuck. I'm terrified of heights.'

'You're not the only one,' Megan said, running alongside. 'I can't even climb up to the second rung of a ladder.'

'Then we're going to have to grab him before he goes too high.' Bella sprinted as fast as she could, lurching towards the dog, missing him as he sprang forward, as nimble as a mountain goat, up the jagged rock face. She and Megan watched in frozen horror as it seemed to dawn on him, when he was about two thirds of the way up, that he was stuck and couldn't get down. Neither could he reach his ball. He turned around and looked in their direction, as if willing them to do something.

Megan and Bella exchanged glances. Bella could see that Megan wasn't in any rush to climb up the rocks and neither was she.

'It's okay, Teddy!' she shouted, trying to keep her tone as calm as possible. 'Good boy! We're coming to get you!'

'Well, I'm not,' Megan argued, her old self returning.

'Er, I think you are,' Bella said. 'You're the one who threw the ball over there.'

'Thanks for the reminder.'

The little dog started whimpering.

'He probably remembers the last time he got stuck up there, when he got hurt,' Megan said, panic entering her voice.

'Which is why we have to get him down as soon as we can, before he does something silly.' Bella surveyed the beach. 'Shame we're the only ones here,' she said, half to herself. 'I'm going to have to begin climbing.' She took a deep breath and, focused on what she was doing, stepped onto the first rock.

'Just don't look down,' Megan advised.

'I wasn't planning to.'

Bella climbed higher and higher, stopping every so often to take deep calming breaths. She swallowed, trying to stave off the panic that was threatening to overcome her. She'd almost reached the little dog when he seemed to become more fretful and started to climb higher.

'Don't move, Teddy. Stay still, there's a good boy,' Bella said, in the calmest voice she could manage. Why had she even thought this would be a good idea?

'You all right up there?' Megan shouted.

'No, I'm not,' Bella replied through gritted teeth. She reached up towards Teddy, but her fingers wouldn't quite reach him. She tried once again, but it was no use. 'He's too far away!' she called, aware that she was running out of options.

'Hang on then, I'm coming!'

Bella glanced down, instantly wishing she hadn't as a wave of nausea swept over her. She could see Megan gingerly making her way up the cliff face. What if Megan couldn't reach him either? Bella took a deep breath and tried to remain calm, concentrating on soothing Teddy.

Megan reached her, slightly out of puff. 'I can't believe I'm doing this,' she said, her voice trembling with fear. 'I don't think I can get down now.'

Neither did Bella, but they were stuck here now and if they didn't do something soon the dog was going to panic. She was terrified he would jump. The thought gave her vertigo and she clung to a rock as tightly as her hands would let her. 'We still haven't reached Teddy yet and we can't think about going down without him.'

'We can't go down at all at the moment. We have to be brave and just do this,' Megan insisted. 'You try to move higher while I stay here.'

'What's that supposed to achieve?'

'I could grab Teddy if he tries to run down.'

'Good luck with that,' she said realising that Teddy was as frozen with fear as they were.

She needed to work out how to get them all safely down to the beach and concentrated on placing one foot above the other in the little nooks and crannies of the rock face. 'He's on a bigger ledge than I expected,' she called back to Megan, as she drew closer to Teddy. She took a deep breath and stretching her free arm up, managed to touch him. If she could just get hold of him now and somehow stay next to him, maybe they could call for help from there? With an effort, she hoisted herself up and was able to lean across the grassy ledge to where he was standing. 'You're all right,' she said, stroking his trembling body.

'Well done!' Megan shouted. 'Hang on to him, won't you?'

She wasn't going to let go of Teddy, or the ledge. In fact, she wasn't sure what to do next. 'Phone Jools,' Bella said as calmly as she could. 'I'll give you her number.'

'Ahh, I didn't actually bring my phone.'

Hiding her disappointment, Bella wondered whether she could climb to the top and on to the headland, Bella looked up, immediately becoming dizzy. She heard panting behind her and tentatively glanced over her shoulder to see Megan approaching. Bella wasn't sure now that insisting Megan should help was a good idea. The girl had guts, and she liked her even more for trying, but two of them stuck with Teddy wasn't going to get them off the cliff.

'Why is no one on the beach apart from us?' Megan yelled.

Bella indicated a steel-grey weather front moving over the channel towards them. 'That's probably why.'

'Great,' Megan grumbled, slipping a few inches, sending small pieces of rock tumbling to the beach below.

'Careful,' Bella said, grabbing her arm and holding her until she found her footing again. 'I don't want to have to rescue you, too.'

Megan reached her and clung on. 'I've already broken a few

nails. And,' she said, raising her designer eyebrows at Bella, 'by the look on your face, I doubt you'll be rescuing anyone, including Teddy.' Her left foot slipped again and she whimpered. 'Have you any idea how we're supposed to get him down? I'm tired and that stormy weather will probably wash us off this rock.'

Bella didn't relish the prospect of staying there much longer. She took a deep breath, wishing she'd never offered to take Teddy out for a walk.

'Is that a fishing boat coming in to shore, do you think?' Megan asked, her fingertips white from clinging on to Bella.

Bella focused on the distant boat. 'It looks like it,' she said, hopefully. 'It's painted red and white, isn't it?'

Megan squinted out to sea. 'Hang on. Yes, it is. Why? Is that good?'

'Hopefully. I think it's Tony's fishing boat. Jack was going out with him.' She could feel the relief, calming her slightly. 'I have an idea.' She carefully pushed her right hand into her jacket pocket, reaching for her mobile. She took it out and found Jack's number. It rang for what seemed like hours, but was probably only seconds, until he answered.

'Bella, hi!' he said shouting above the boat's engine noise. She sensed from his tone that he was still a little awkward after their close encounter a few days earlier.

'Oh Jack, I'm so glad you've answered,' she said, not caring that he would hear how frightened she was.

'Bella? Where are you? Has something happened? Is it Betty?' He wasn't giving her time to reply.

'No, Jack... please, just listen. Megan and I are stuck up the cliff at the beach.'

There was a pause. 'What are you doing up there?' he said. 'You're terrified of heights.'

She told him about taking Teddy for a walk and him chasing the ball. 'And now all three of us are stuck and don't know how to get down. The tide has come in too,' she said, as the realisation dawned on her, that even if they did get down in one piece, they still had to get the dog to dry land.

'Hey, it's going to be fine,' Jack soothed. 'The first thing to do is not panic.'

'And the second?'

'I'm not sure yet.' She could hear him speaking with Tony. 'We're going to bring the boat in as close as we can. If you can get lower down with Teddy then do, but if not, just wait for me. Okay? Don't try anything heroic.'

She was past trying anything at all. 'Yes, please hurry,' she said, trying not to cry with relief. She cleared her throat after he ended the call. 'Jack is on that fishing boat and he's going to try and rescue us.'

Megan sighed heavily. 'I knew he was a hero the moment I set eyes on him,' she said, relaxing her grip slightly.

Bella cuddled Teddy as best she could with her free arm. 'He's shivering, poor little guy.'

'Should we try and cover him with something?'

'Good idea.' She carefully unravelled her scarf and wound it awkwardly around the little dog. 'It might make him feel better,' she said, wishing there was something she could do to help her and Megan. Her teeth were chattering and her jaw was becoming sore from trying to stop them. 'We just have to stay as calm as we can until Jack gets here,' she added, as much to reassure herself as Megan.

'I hope he gets here soon because I'm bloody freezing,' Megan moaned. 'I wish I'd never thrown that bloody ball.'

'Stop blaming yourself. These things happen,' Bella said, even though it had been Megan's fault. After all, she specifically told her not to throw the ball at the rocks. 'Anyway, knowing Jack, he won't take long to get here. He's very clever at anything outdoorsy.' She hoped she was right. He'd never had to rescue her from a cliff ledge before

'I was wondering,' Megan said. 'Should I try and climb to the top, do you think?'

Bella looked up without thinking. Again, her world turned on its axis. 'That was a bad idea,' she groaned. 'I have no idea if you can find a way up there, but I can't see one.'

Megan looked pensive, scanning the rock face back and forth. 'Maybe we're looking at this the wrong way,' she said. 'Instead of going up, we should go to the right or the left. Take our time getting to the top.'

Bella gave it some thought. She had a point. Neither of them could hang on much longer. She looked around but couldn't see any way that they could go. 'Jack did say to wait, and I think that's our safest bet.'

'We got up, though,' Megan argued. 'Why the hell can't we get back down?'

'Fine,' Bella said. 'I'm going to try again.' She took one step and the rock gave way beneath her feet. Stones cascaded down, several of them giving Megan glancing blows. She shrieked, startling Teddy. Bella clung to him, making soothing noises as the rocks streamed noisily below. 'Okay, that's it, I'm not going anywhere. I'm waiting for Jack.'

A man's voice bellowed from below. They looked down tentatively to see Alessandro, waving up at them. Cupping his hands either side of his mouth, he called, 'Bella, you are okay? You wish for me to climb up to you?'

'It's not just us,' Bella called back. 'We've got a dog and we don't know how to get him down.'

'I get help,' Alessandro called. 'You wait, I come back soon.'

Before Bella could tell him about Jack, he turned and ran off.

'For pity's sake,' Megan moaned. 'Who does he think is going to come and help us? The coastguard, I suppose, or the fire brigade. Oh hell, imagine the photos.'

'It'll be fine. I'm sure Jack will be here before anyone else,' Bella said hopefully, scanning the sea to try and gauge how close he was.

Megan suddenly giggled. 'You do know you're going to laugh about this one day?'

Bella wasn't sure about that. She couldn't imagine ever laughing about something that had terrified her quite so much. But to keep the peace, and keep Megan's mind off the fact that they were holding on tightly to a rock face, she nodded. 'Yes, you're probably right,' she said. 'But I think it's going to be a long while.'

They waited, trying to remain calm, telling each other jokes to pass the time, watching as the boat came closer. Eventually, Bella spotted Jack, waving at them, and then she could hear his voice. She waved back, relief washing through her. Thank God he'd been close enough to take her call.

'I phoned Alessandro!' Jack shouted. 'He's getting my surfboard from the cottage and is bringing it down here.'

'What the hell is he doing that for?' Megan asked, frowning.

'Shush,' Bella said, quietly. 'I don't care how he does this, I just want to get down. So listen to what he has to say.' She turned her attention to Jack. 'Just tell us what you want us to do when you're ready.'

Alessandro ran into view, carrying Jack's bright orange surfboard. Bella and Megan watched while he pushed it out towards the boat and held it as Jack jumped into the water.

She heard Jack tell him to keep the surfboard close to the bottom of the cliff and saw Alessandro hand him what looked like a rucksack. Bella wasn't sure why he'd been carrying it but maybe there was something inside it that would be useful. The girls waited silently while Jack made quick work of climbing the rock face.

'I think he's done this sort of thing before,' Megan said, smiling for the first time since their escapade had begun.

'You could be right,'

'Hi, girls,' Jack said, looking very comfortable as he joined them. Reaching Teddy, he checked him briefly. 'You poor little thing,' he said, giving the dog a one-armed cuddle. Teddy seemed ecstatic to see him, his whole body wagged with delight. Bella knew how he felt. 'I can see you're all freezing,' he said, bringing the rucksack around to his front. 'I'm going to put Teddy into this rucksack and zip it up slightly to hold his body inside.' He slowly lifted the dog, and with a bit of effort, slipped him inside. 'Can you help me get my arms through the straps?' he asked Bella, carefully pulling the bag around, talking calmly to Teddy.

'Of course.' She was happy to agree to anything that would get them down.

'That's it,' he said, quietly, once the rucksack was secure. 'Hey, little guy,' he said, when Teddy started panting. 'You're going to be fine. We'll have you home in no time.' He smiled at Bella. 'You okay for a bit?'

'I suppose so.' She gave him a tearful smile. 'I'm just glad Teddy's okay. She wondered how she was going to break the news of Teddy's adventure to Mrs Jones. She probably wouldn't be allowed to take him out for another walk and wouldn't blame Mrs Jones for being furious, considering she'd done the very thing she had expressly asked Bella not to do.

'I'll be back as quick as I can,' he said.

Bella and Megan watched his easy descent. He was soon at

the bottom, where Alessandro was waiting on the surfboard. Sitting astride it, they paddled to the beach, where Alessandro got off and lifted Teddy from the rucksack.

'Look,' Bella said, watching the dog run up the beach towards the bookshop. 'He's taking him back to Mrs Jones. Isn't he clever?'

'Isn't it sickening when they make it all look so easy?' Megan said. 'Maybe we should try and get down by ourselves.'

Bella had been considering doing the same thing. She was used to being capable and didn't fancy waiting for Jack to rescue her as if she was some sort of nursery-story princess.

'Urgh, I want to, but it's not as if we've managed to even move a foot so far.' She peered down and saw Jack already paddling the surfboard back to the bottom of the cliffs. He hooked the ankle strap over a narrow rock and began his second ascent.

'Shall we try to come down to you?' she asked, willing him to say no.

'You're probably better waiting for me to help you,' he said. 'Your muscles must be cold by now and we don't want either of you falling.' He waved at her to stay put and reached them so quickly it made Bella wonder why she was making such a fuss. Then again, she was scared of heights and Jack wasn't.

'Who's coming down with me first?'

'Take Megan,' Bella insisted. After all, Megan was a guest, and a celeb, and she certainly didn't need the girl's injury or death on her conscience.

Jack spoke quietly to Megan, telling her to follow exactly where he put his hands and feet and slowly they started their descent. It took a lot longer than when he'd gone down with Teddy. Soon though, Bella was relieved to see Megan sitting on the back of the surfboard. She smiled to herself, seeing Megan's arms wrapped around Jack's waist. Even in times of stress, Megan was still able to make the most of any opportunity with a man.

Jack paddled them over to the shore where Alessandro helped Megan off and wrapped a towel around her.

Finally, Jack was on his way back for her. Bella ached from the effort of being on a narrow ledge trying not to look up or down for so long. She was getting cramp in her legs and her whole body trembled from the cold. Feeling awkward that he was having to rescue her, she reminded herself that if she wanted to get down, this was her only option.

'You alright up there?' Jack said when he reached her. He put one arm around her. 'You're freezing. Don't worry, this won't take long. You saw what I did with Megan?' She nodded. 'Just take your time and slowly put one foot down at a time, finding a place to grip as you go.'

She tried to do as he asked but found that her body wouldn't respond. Her heart pounded hard against her ribs. 'I can't move,' she whispered. 'I really can't.'

'Take a moment,' he said gently. 'Once you begin, you'll be fine. I'm right next to you, so you won't fall.'

'Promise?' She was barely able to force the words out of her mouth.

'You know I won't let anything happen to you.' He rested a palm between her shoulders, the heat of his hand calming her slightly. 'Shall we go then?' He gave her a reassuring smile. 'You can do this, trust me.'

At first, she didn't think she could. But one look at Jack's determined expression gave her the confidence to try and do what he'd asked. Taking a deep breath, she shakily moved one foot down. Finding a firm footing, she lowered the other foot.

Jack was right next to her. 'You're doing really well.'

She glanced at him, his confidence boosting her own. Relaxing slightly, she lowered her foot without checking it was secure and slipped. She screamed as she dropped and Jack grabbed hold of her jacket and held on tightly. 'Don't panic,' he said. 'Find your footing, take your time.'

Within five minutes, she realised her foot was wet. They'd reached the bottom and she was standing on a rock, ankle deep in the sea, which was rougher than it had been earlier.

Jack put his arm around her shoulders. 'The storm will be with us in a few minutes,' he said. 'We need to get you home and into a hot shower.'

'I feel such a fool,' she said, tearful with relief. Her legs were shaky despite her exhilaration to have made it – with Jack's help. 'But I had to go after Teddy.'

Jack turned her to face him. 'What else could you have done? You would never leave anybody in trouble without trying to help them, despite how frightened you might be. It's your natural instinct to do the right thing.' He pulled her to him and gave her a tight hug. 'You're trembling,' he said, kissing the top of her head. 'You gave me such a fright when I saw you up there. I know how terrified of heights you are.'

She put her arms round his waist, resting her head on his warm chest as her breathing slowly began to return to normal. She hadn't realised quite how terrified she'd been until now. She wished she could stop shaking quite so much. 'Thanks for being there for us, Jack. I really appreciate it, and I know Megan does too.'

'I was only too pleased to help.' He looked down. Bella followed his line of vision and realised that he wanted her to get on the surfboard.

'Take my hand,' he said, stepping down and sitting astride. 'That's right.'

He waited patiently, holding her hand to steady her while she put her leg over and settled behind him. 'Put your arms around my waist and let's get going.'

A wave crashed against the surfboard, pushing it against the rocks and narrowly missing crushing her leg.

'The tide really has picked up,' he said, paddling towards the beach.

She held on tightly and closed her eyes, resting her head against his muscular back. It was a relief to finally relax, despite being soaking wet and colder than she could ever remember. She relished the heat of his body against hers.

'Nearly there, Bella,' he said, over his shoulder. 'Are you still up for the bonfire beach-party tonight? Don't feel you have to help, you've had a traumatic day.'

'Of course, I'm not going to miss it,' she said. 'And I want to help.' It was the least she could do in return for him rescuing her, Megan and Teddy. 'I've been looking forward to it. I know Megan has too. In fact, the entire village will probably show up, so it should be great fun.' She tickled his side.

Jack laughed. 'Hey, stop that. You know I'm ticklish.'

They reached the beach and Jack lifted her from the surfboard as Alessandro unfolded a large towel and wrapped it around her. 'Here is one for you,' he said, handing Jack a smaller towel. 'Sorry, it is all I find.'

'We need to get you girls home,' Jack said, before turning to Alessandro. 'You'd better go and help Sacha with the food for the party,' he added. 'Thanks for your help, mate, I'll catch up with you later – let you know how the girls are getting on.'

On shaky legs, Bella accompanied Megan and Jack back to her cottage. 'Go up and have a shower, Megan,' she insisted. 'I'll light the fire down here for when you're done.'

Megan ran up the stairs. 'Help yourself to some dry clothes from my bedroom,' Bella yelled after her. 'It's the one on the right at the top of the stairs.'

'You go up, too,' Jack said. 'Get those wet clothes off and wrap yourself up. I'll light the fire and make some hot drinks for when you're both back down.'

Bella was grateful for his thoughtfulness. 'But what about you?'

Jack shook his head and smiled. 'I'm used to the cold water, don't forget. You're not. Now, for once, go and do as you're told.'

Once they'd had their showers and changed, and were having a cup of tea, Jack said, 'Don't forget we've still got the bonfire to sort out.'

'In this weather?' Megan looked horrified at the thought of going back to the beach in the wind and rain.

'According to the forecast, the weather's going to clear up. The storm should have passed by the time we light the fire at seven thirty.'

Bella suddenly realised no one had thought to tell Megan's manager or Lexi where she was. 'Will they be looking for you?' she asked. 'Where did you say you were going today?'

'It'll be fine,' Megan reassured her. 'I told them I was meeting you, so no one will be waiting for me to get back, which,' she laughed, 'is probably a good thing under the circumstances.'

Jack's mobile pinged. He read the message and nodded. 'Alessandro said to tell you that he delivered Teddy to Mrs Jones and explained what had happened.'

Bella grimaced, waiting to hear what she had said next.

'It's fine,' Jack smiled at her. 'Apparently, she was perfectly fine and doesn't hold anyone responsible. She knows how naughty Teddy can be when he's chasing his ball.'

'That's a relief,' Bella said taking a sip of her hot drink. Closing her eyes, she tried not to think of the state her hands must be in. She had had enough of drama for one day and would worry about them another time.

15

Several hours later, calmer and much warmer, having drunk several hot drinks, Jack, Bella and Megan were ready to start preparations for the bonfire party. Alessandro had joined them.

'We're lucky that it's a low tide tonight,' Jack said. 'It means that if we start preparing the bonfire now we could build it fairly close to the wall. We don't want it to be too big. I had a call from my friend who's supplying us with the fireworks,' he went on. 'He's bringing them down just after six. I thought we could set them up further down the beach. It shouldn't take long.'

'Sounds good,' Bella said. 'As long as they're a safe distance from everyone.'

'He's bringing buckets,' Jack said. 'We fill them with sand, stick the fireworks in, and light them when we're ready. The sand can be poured back onto the beach afterwards.'

'Perfect,' Bella said, unsurprised that Jack had thought everything through so thoroughly. 'And these are the silent fireworks? I've never seen them used before.'

'What an awesome idea,' Megan said. 'My mum hates fireworks because she's got two little dogs. I've got a friend back home who has a couple of ponies who have to be taken into their stables when people set them off around bonfire night and for wedding receptions. There's a venue near where she lives. She was saying how much worse it seems to be getting.'

'I know,' Jack agreed. 'The worst thing is that it's not one night, it's a week or two before and after. It's not as if you can plan what to do with the animals, especially outdoors. It must be horrendous for farmers,' he said. 'Silent fireworks are a great idea. I just wish everyone would buy them.'

'Maybe our display will persuade them,' Bella said. 'Are they expensive?'

'I didn't have to pay for them,' Jack said. 'It was the assistant manager, Charlie, who works at the Sea Breeze Hotel. We had a drink in the pub a few weeks back when I mentioned trying to find some. He told me he had been trying to persuade the owners of the Sea Breeze to have a party but replace the fireworks with silent ones. They weren't sure it was a good idea, or whether they'd work as well, or be much fun. He said he'd source them and arrange a display and if they thought it was worthwhile, next year they could use them for wedding receptions and New Year celebrations.'

'That's brilliant,' Bella cheered, liking Charlie even more for being so forward-thinking. 'It'll make all the difference to the villagers.'

'And they can all come to the party tonight and give their opinion, and it won't even cost them anything.'

'You are clever, Jack Collins.' Bella gave him a cheeky smile. 'I might have known you'd do something to benefit everybody else.'

'I won't miss the loud bangs,' Megan said. 'I think it's outdated, having to listen to that ear-splitting noise. My father said last year that the whole house was shaking, the explosions were so loud around where we live. He thinks they should be banned and I agree.'

Aware that time was speeding by, Bella asked Jack what he wanted them to do.

'I suppose the first thing would be to collect wood for the bonfire,' he said, as they went outside and began walking along the boardwalk. He pointed to a spot on the sand in the middle of the beach between the cliffs, where he had recently helped her and Megan down, and the red and white painted lighthouse to the left of them. 'I think somewhere in the middle,' he said. 'That way, everyone along the boardwalk will have a clear view and we can set out the buckets at a decent distance from the railings where the locals might be standing.'

'Sounds good.'

'Sacha's making hot dogs, toffee apples and drinks for the party, at five pounds a pop. Two pounds for children and pensioners.'

'What sort of drinks?' asked Megan.

Alessandro thought for a moment. 'It is a warm drink,' he said, glancing at Jack for input. 'I cannot think its name. It is made with wine.'

'Do you mean mulled wine?' Bella suggested, hoping that was the case. She hadn't sampled any since Sacha's Christmas party at the café the previous year, and it had been delicious.

'Yes,' he smiled. 'Is good, she tells me.' He looked at Megan. 'And the children they have blackcurrant juice, also warm. Is good, I think, don't you?'

'Yes, that's a brilliant choice,' Megan said. Linking arms with Bella, she gazed from her to Jack. 'This is such a cool place to live,' she said. 'I'm definitely going to come back as soon as I can.'

Bella was pleased. She was relieved that she and Megan had got over their differences and were friends.

'Hey, you lot.'

They all looked towards the bottom of the hill to see Lexi running towards them waving a large brown envelope excitedly.

'I wonder what that is?' Bella asked Jack, exchanging glances with him.

Megan gasped. 'She sent it. I bet this is the magazine with my interview and those photos that were taken the other day.'

Lexi reached them and handed the envelope to Megan. 'This came by courier a few minutes ago.'

They watched as Megan tore it open and peeked inside, giving an excited scream. 'It is my interview. Come on, let's get out of the wind and go to the café to have a proper look.'

Without argument all of them raced to the café. Jack got to the door first and held it open for them to go inside.

'There's a free table, at the back,' Bella shouted, pointing.

Sacha looked up from taking an order and shook her head, smiling. 'What's happened?' She finished what she was doing and walked over to join them.

They each took a seat, staring wide-eyed at Megan. She pulled out the magazine and held it up for them to see a stunning photo of her taken on the beach with Jack emerging from the sea in the background, his tanned muscular body dripping with water.

Bella's stomach did a somersault.

'Bloody hell Jack, you look gorgeous. I don't look too bad though, do I?'

'You look amazing, Megan,' Bella said, unable to take her eyes from Jack's glistening six pack in the photo as he pushed his hair out of his eyes, seemingly oblivious to the camera. He was a natural.

'They're more appealing than the ones in the paper taken by the paps,' she said, raising an eyebrow at Jack.

He coughed. 'Never mind that. What about the photos of the café, your antique shop, Jools' grandma's bookshop and Lexi's cottages?'

Megan licked her finger and quickly ran through the pages. 'Centre spread,' she said, flattening the magazine onto the table so they could all have a good look.

Bella leaned forward and saw that the larger photos were all of Megan, which was only right as the feature had been about her, but she smiled to see that each of their businesses had been included in smaller photos. 'What do they say in the interview?'

Megan began to read the article. As Bella listened to her relating to the journalist how difficult she had been during the original photoshoot in London and how grateful she was to Bella and her friends for looking after her during her extended stay on the island, she realised that she had misread the girl. Megan wasn't as shallow as she had initially seemed. She had certainly done her best to make amends in ensuring that each of the group and their businesses had received a mention.

'It was generous of you to include us all,' Lexi said. 'Thanks, Megan.'

Megan blushed. It was the first time Bella had seen her looking so awkward. 'It was the least I could do after you've all looked after me so well.'

'I'm going to use this in my next promotion for this place,' Sacha said.

Jack checked his watch. 'We need to get a move on,' he said. 'Could you two stay here and help Sacha make the food, and do anything else she needs you to,' he said, looking at Megan and Alessandro. 'That's if you want to?'

Megan nodded, beaming at him and linking arms with Alessandro. 'I'd love to. This is such fun. We'd love to, wouldn't we, Alessandro?' she said, giggling.

Bella smiled at Jack, unable to wipe away the picture of him from the magazine. 'What would you like me to do? Fetch the wood, I suppose?'

'Yes, please,' he said. 'We could go together. Can we borrow your car again, Lexi? We can get some logs from a farmer I know. He keeps them in the barn, so they'll be dry and should burn well.'

Bella nodded, pleased to have something to do to take her mind off the photos, even if she would be spending it with Jack. She wondered if he would mention the incident earlier, when she'd been holding on to him as they'd sat astride his surfboard, but he didn't say anything.

* * *

As they drove up the hill in Lexi's car, Bella said, 'Is there anything else we should have thought of. For tonight, I mean?'

'No, I don't think so.' Jack thought for a moment. 'Firelighters,' he said. 'We'll need to light the fire with something, won't we?'

'It would help,' she laughed. 'Isn't it funny how it's always the most obvious things that people forget?'

'I know, but we are doing this at very short notice,' Jack said with a grin. 'We'll stop at the garage at the top of the hill before getting the wood. They sell firelighters, and those long matches. We can ask them if there's anything else we might need.'

They drove on in silence for a couple of minutes. Bella spotted him giving her sideways glances, and could see something was on his mind. She waited in the car while he went into the garage shop, wondering what he was thinking. He returned with a bag that looked rather more filled than she would have expected.

'Now I think we have everything,' he said, grinning.

They reached the farm a few minutes later and after a quick word with the farmer, parked the car, folded the back seats down to accommodate the logs, and went into the barn.

'Jack, is there something you want to say?' Bella asked.

He stared at her for a second, his face hard to read in the shadowy barn, and she was disappointed when he shook his head. 'No, it's fine,' he said, starting to load various sized logs into the back of the car.

She didn't ask again and once they had enough logs, they drove in silence back to the boardwalk where Jack parked and took hold of her hand.

'You okay?'

She thought it was an odd question to ask, but presumed he was referring to her being stuck on the rocks earlier. 'Yes, thanks. I'm fine.'

'Good, I'm glad.'

He looked at her a moment longer, still holding her hand, their eyes locked, then he abruptly let go and got out of the car. They took the logs from the boot straight on to the beach, working silently until they had used made a neat pile.

'I think we need another load, don't you?' asked Jack.

Bella nodded, it wouldn't be much of a bonfire, otherwise. They returned to the car and drove back to the farm for another load. She didn't mind one bit. She was enjoying being with Jack, even though he seemed a little pensive. It was just nice to spend time alone with him.

'Bella,' he said, breaking the silence, his voice quiet as they loaded the car for the second time.

She stiffened, concerned at his serious tone. 'Yes?'

He turned to face her. Taking her by the arms, he checked over his shoulder that the farmer wasn't within earshot. 'You know the other day, when I… well, when we kissed and then you stopped me.'

'Sort of,' she said, though she'd barely thought of anything else. 'Go on.'

'How do you feel about me?' He studied her face, waiting for her to reply.

Bella couldn't lie to him. He knew her too well for her to get away with that. Besides, he was her friend and he lived in her house. The last thing she needed or wanted was for them to fall out or for there to be any tension between them.

'I like you, Jack,' she admitted. 'I think you know that I do.'

'And I feel the same about you, as I'm sure you know,' he said. 'I know that the first time we kissed, Sacha took it badly. I understand why she reacted like that. She was trying to protect us both, but we're adults now, and I'm not the same person I was when I was with Nicki. Sacha will understand. She'd want us to be happy. What do you think?'

Had Jack really changed that much? Would Sacha be angry that something might have been going on between Bella and her brother behind her back? She couldn't bear to ruin their friendship.

'I'm not sure,' she said honestly, hating the disappointment in his face. 'What if things don't work out, and Sacha stops speaking to me, and you have to leave the cottage, and…'

'Leave Sacha to me,' he interrupted, gently stroking a strand of hair off her cheek. 'If that's what you're really worried about, I'll talk to her.'

Bella decided to trust him. 'Are you sure that'll be the right thing to do? I wouldn't want to upset her.'

'I'll do my best to reassure her that I'd never hurt you.'

Her insides tumbled with a mix of nerves and joy. She

believed him and wanted to take a chance. A chance on her and Jack.

They arrived at the boardwalk and as Jack parked the car, Bella spotted Nicki walking towards them. Her heart plunged. 'Looks like you've got a visitor,' she said, opening the car door. 'I'll unload the logs and take them down to the beach.'

'Wait,' Jack grabbed Bella's wrist. 'Do you really think there's still something between me and Nicki? After that farce with Oliver Whimsy the other night?' He shook his head. 'Seriously, Bella?'

She could see he was angry, or maybe disappointed, and didn't like it. 'You've been on and off with her for years, Jack,' she said tightly, as Nicki drew closer. 'You need to sort things out with her, once and for all.'

'I didn't even know she was still here,' he said. 'I thought she'd left when that Whimsy bloke did.'

'Exactly.' Bella pulled away and got out of the car. 'She's unpredictable, Jack. I don't want to have to deal with her popping up, if you're serious about us having a relationship.'

'I am.' He got out and opened the boot of the car. 'I'll speak to her right now.'

'Oliver Whimsy didn't look very happy when I saw him.'

Jack frowned at her. 'You saw him?' he said. 'When?'

'Never mind that now.' Bella indicated that Nicki was almost at the car.

'Jack!' she called, giving him a wave, ignoring Bella altogether.

He turned to face Nicki, his face grimly determined, and grabbing an armful of logs, Bella descended the granite steps to the beach and left them to it, the sound of Nicki's bossy voice ringing in her ears. She was her complete opposite, Bella thought, dropping the logs on the sand. She was elegant and groomed and brilliant at her job. Why would Jack find Bella attractive? Yet, he clearly did. The memory of their kiss made her face heat up, even as she heard Nicki's voice rising in the air.

'You're talking rubbish now, Jack,' she said. 'I don't know why you won't discuss this sensibly.'

'Because I have nothing left to say to you.' Jack's voice was weary.

Unable to resist returning to the car, Bella went back up the steps to see Jack marching towards the café. 'Bugger,' she muttered. Now she was stuck with Nicki.

'What?' Nicki snapped as soon as she saw her. She folded her arms across the chest and glared at Bella.

'Nothing,' said Bella.

'You seem to be very interested in Jack all of a sudden.' Nicki stared at her. 'I'll bet it's your fault he's behaving like this.'

Bella had never interfered in Jack's relationship with Nicki, even though she'd never liked the woman, but she'd had enough of her.

'If I am, it's none of your business,' she said. 'You really need to decide who you want to be with – Oliver Whimsy, or Jack. You can't mess people around like you've been doing, it's just not fair. And anyway,' she said, on a roll, wishing she could shut up because she was going to get herself into trouble with Jack, and because she knew Nicki was not someone to be messed with, 'Jack's told you he's got no intention of returning to London, yet you're still chasing him. I don't get it.'

'It's not for you to get,' Nicki sneered. 'Why don't you butt out? Just because you don't have a relationship of your own to focus on, you think you can tell me what to do with my life.' She started to walk away, her stilettos click-clacking, leaving Bella shaking with annoyance, then came back.

'For your information, I'm not interested in Jack.' She gave a sarcastic laugh. 'Let's be honest, you two are far more suited.' She gave the cottage a look of disdain before focusing her attention back on Bella. 'He can hardly afford to give me the big house, the nanny and the decent car that I want. I'm only interested in marrying someone with prospects. And, much as I like being with Jack for the,' she giggled, 'more *intimate* side of a relationship, I'll only marry for money. And, let's be honest, whatever you think of Jack, he has precious little of that.'

'You really are despicable,' Bella said through gritted teeth, pushing away the thought of the two of them being intimate. 'In fact, you're vile. I can't understand what Jack ever saw in you.' She knew she was being as revolting as Nicki, but couldn't help herself. This horrible woman, who thought so highly of herself, was criticising Jack, the kindest, most thoughtful man Bella knew, and she was not going to get away with saying such dreadful things about him. 'I've known him my entire life and he is far more of a man than you deserve, or could ever handle.'

Nicki looked astonished. Her cosmetically enhanced eyebrows almost disappeared into her slick fringe. She narrowed her eyes and stepped towards Bella, towering above her. 'Well, well, little Miss Antique Shop has a secret crush on Jack.' She gave a sardonic laugh. 'Does he know?'

Furious with Nicki for seeing through her, Bella retaliated immediately. 'How I feel about him is none of your damn business. You don't want him any more. Or is it that he's thoroughly sick of you? Maybe that's why you're still hanging around. Either way, how I feel about him is nothing to do with you.'

'I knew it! You're in love with him.'

'So what if I am?'

'Well?'

Bella swung around. 'Mum! I didn't see you there.'

Her mum smiled. 'Go on, sweetheart, tell Nicki how you feel about Jack.'

'Yes, go on, Bella,' Jack said, joining them, staring intently at her. 'Please tell Nicki how you feel about me.'

'Well, I—' she began, feeling cornered. She didn't know what to say, or do, and didn't like being told to declare her feelings in front of them all. She chewed her lower lip thoughtfully.

Jack took Bella's hand in his, staring at her as if no one else existed. 'Bella,' he said, his voice gentle. 'I want you to know that I'm falling in love with you. Scrap that,' he corrected. 'I *am* in love with you.' He looked at Nicki. 'I'm sorry, Nicki, but I think deep down there's always been a part of me that's been in love with Bella. Ever since the night I kissed her, when she was sixteen.'

Bella bit her lower lip. Hearing him declare his feelings in a way that no one could argue with, was incredible. She'd never felt about anyone the way she felt about Jack, but she'd kept her feelings hidden for so long that it felt odd admitting them to anyone else.

'Bella?' her mum said. 'Say something.'

She rested her hand on his cheek. 'The thing is, Jack,' she said. 'I feel exactly the same way about you.'

16

Bella sat on her bed and closed her eyes, trying to make sense of everything that had happened. Thirteen years of acting a certain way and keeping her feelings to herself, and now they were finally out in the open.

After Nicki had stalked away – hopefully right off the island – they'd gone to the café to break the news to Sacha. As Jack had predicted, she'd been thrilled for them – though sad that Bella had never confided her feelings about Jack.

'I know I reacted badly to seeing you kissing my brother that time, at the beach,' she'd said, throwing her arms round Bella, almost in tears. 'I had no idea you still felt so strongly about him. You should have said something.'

They'd both cried a little, and talked it out, while her mother dabbed her eyes with a tissue, and Jack tried to hold Bella's hand.

Afterwards, Jack had gone back to the beach to finish setting up the bonfire, while Bella popped back to the cottage to freshen up, but time was marching on, and the party was approaching.

'Finally, I have you to myself,' Jack said, when she joined him back at the beach, where he was presiding over the bonfire. 'Can I kiss you again?'

'I can't think of anything I'd prefer,' Bella admitted, unable to think clearly with his muscular body pressed against hers. She felt herself melting into him as their lips met, and slid her arms around his neck.

'Hey, what are you two doing down there?' Megan giggled.

They looked up to see her leaning over the railings, amused to see them together.

'If you've got nothing better to do,' Jack said, smiling, 'go and knock on some doors and ask for more logs. We haven't got quite enough yet.'

'Good idea,' Bella murmured, as Jack pulled her back into his arms and continued kissing her. 'Stop it,' she giggled. 'We're supposed to be getting ready for this party.'

'I'd rather do this.' He kissed her neck and made her insides go wobbly. 'I've waited a very long time for this to happen and I'm not going to stop for a while yet. Not unless you want me to.'

She didn't. Pressing herself against him, Bella lost herself in the joy of kissing him, only to be distracted by a car pulling up on the boardwalk. Jack groaned and pulled away from Bella. 'The fireworks have arrived,' he said. 'Can we continue this later?'

* * *

Bella stood, wrapped up in her thickest coat, scarf, woolly bobble hat and gloves, watching as Jack and his friend Mike, and Alessandro, took their places, ready to start the firework display. Jack turned to address the gathered crowd.

'Firstly,' he said, his face lit by the glow of lights from the boardwalk as he glanced briefly at Bella, causing her stomach to flip over at the promise of what was to come later, 'I'd like to thank all of you who have helped to make this bonfire party possible.' There was a loud burst of applause.

Bella smiled at the people around her, grateful to be a part of this wonderful community. The bonfire was roaring, the air was filled with mouth-watering aromas, thanks to Sacha's food display, and she was surrounded by people she loved.

'Secondly, as I'm sure most of you know, this is not only a celebration of Guy Fawkes Night, but also a trial for Mike's soundless fireworks,' Jack continued. 'We're hoping that you enjoy this evening without the usual bangs, and that you'll consider using them in future, and recommend them to your friends.'

'Hear, hear,' shouted one of the locals. 'It's about time.'

A few people clapped. Jack nodded. 'My sentiments exactly, thank you.' He raised one arm, holding a lit taper. 'Everyone please, let's have fun tonight. Alessandro, Mike... when you're ready?'

As they lit the first set of rockets to the delight of the onlookers gathered on the boardwalk, Megan walked up and linked her arm through Bella's. 'This is amazing,' she said, beaming at her. 'Thank you so much for inviting me back.'

'I'm thrilled you came,' Bella said with a smile, glad that Megan was clearly enjoying herself. 'Maybe you'll come to visit us again after this. I know we didn't get off to the best start in London but I've really enjoyed getting to know you.'

'Me, too,' Megan said, hugging Bella tightly. 'I feel like I've gained, not just you as a friend, but a whole new friendship group. To be honest, I've been feeling lonely since I moved to London. It's a completely different lifestyle. I know my manager tries her best to help me integrate but it's not the same as having people you can truly relax with.'

'I can assure you that you'll always have us as friends, and we'll always be pleased to see you.'

'Thank you.' Megan's eyes looked suspiciously shiny.

'Hey,' Lexi shouted, running down the granite steps, closely followed by Jools. 'We were wondering where you two had got to.' They gave a collective gasp as fireworks shot up into the sky, exploding high above them in pinks and blues.

It really was a magical evening and Bella was happy for Jack after all his hard work. Who would have thought only a few short weeks ago, that after years of loving him secretly, they now had a real chance of making a future together?

Lexi stood on the other side of Bella, her arm through hers and, in a low voice, said, 'I've heard whispers about you and Jack Collins, kissing,' she grinned. 'I'm so relieved you two have finally got it together.'

Bella couldn't believe her feelings had been so obvious. 'You knew I liked him?'

'Yes,' Lexi whispered. 'But I like to think I'm more intuitive than the others, so don't worry, I don't think they had a clue. I do think you make a perfect couple, though.'

'Do you really think so?' she asked, smiling as Lexi nodded.

'Anyone who's ever seen you two together would say the same thing. I could tell he'd had the hots for you for years. Jack really is a gem, Bella, but I'm sure you already know that.'

'I do.' For years, she'd been looking for a priceless gem that would change her life, at auctions and house clearances, but all the time the priceless gem had been right under her nose. 'I'm so glad we're making a go of it.' It sounded strange, hearing herself say it out loud. Discussing her feelings for Jack, even to her close friends, was an alien concept to Bella and one she longed to be able to carry on. 'He really is lovely, inside and out.'

'Look,' Jools shouted, pointing at Jack, Mike and Alessandro as they began a countdown and lit three massive fireworks at once.

'Pay attention!' Jack shouted. 'This is your grand finale.'

Everybody clapped and cheered as the fireworks shot into the air and exploded across the sky like tiny lanterns, before slowly falling and disappearing.

A chorus of gasps accompanied the display and Bella was glad the trial run had been a huge success. She spotted Jack emptying the buckets of sand and clearing away the debris before coming towards her followed by Alessandro and Mike.

Reaching her, he took her hand in his. 'What did you think?'

'Incredible,' she said honestly. 'You guys did really well.'

Sacha came over with a tray of glasses filled with mulled wine. 'Drink this,' she said. 'It'll warm you all up.'

Bella took a sip and glanced at Sacha, who gave her a secret smile. Bella grinned back, relieved to be reminded that her friend had no issue with her and Jack being a couple. It was more than she had ever dared hope for.

'As this is going to be Alessandro's first Christmas on the island,' Sacha said, 'tonight has reminded us what fun we can have here. We were wondering whether you'd all like to join us on Christmas Day, for Christmas lunch at the café?'

'I'd love to come,' Bella said, without having to consider the invitation. 'Do you think Mum and Betty could come along too?'

'And me,' Megan said. 'Will I be able to join in?'

'Of course,' Sacha said. 'The more the merrier. Your mum is also very welcome,' Sacha said. 'And we're going to invite Tony the fisherman and his children.'

Jack nodded and lowering his voice said, 'He was telling me on the boat when we were out fishing the other day how difficult last Christmas was without his wife. He'll be glad to not be sitting at home, missing her, and having to put on a brave face.'

'I'll definitely be there,' Lexi said. 'Especially as Dad has decided to go to an artists' retreat in France over Christmas and the New Year.'

'You can always come to me if he ever does that sort of thing,' Bella insisted.

Jack finished his drink and turned to Alessandro and Sacha. 'Why don't you guys go back to the café and count the takings for tonight, then we can decide what to put the money towards before we clear up here.'

He handed the pot of money to Alessandro. 'You two go ahead,' he said. 'I've just got something I want to run by Bella. We won't be long.'

Concerned, Bella kept her smile fixed as Sacha and Alessandro headed off. 'Sounds ominous,' she said, hoping Jack wasn't having second thoughts about their relationship already.

'I just need to show you something,' he reassured her. He took her hand and led her back to the cottage.

'What is it?' she said, wondering why it couldn't wait as he pushed open the door and tugged her over the threshold.

'I just wanted to do this.' Putting his arms around her waist and pulling her tightly against him, he kissed her – slowly at first, and then more passionately.

It was the best surprise.

Bella decided that kissing Jack really was going to be her new favourite pastime.

ACKNOWLEDGMENTS

Thanks to my wonderful editor Tara Loder, to Rose Fox for her proofs and to the entire team at Boldwood Books for being so amazing.

To Alan Reed who entered a competition to name one of the characters in this book. My character Abel Reed was named after his grandson.

To Karen Clarke and Rebecca Baudains for being early readers of this book, thank you for your wonderful suggestions.

Love and thanks to my husband, Rob for everything, my three dogs, Jarvis, Claude and Rudi who make sure I don't spend too long sitting and looking at a screen, and my children, James and Saskia for just being themselves.

To my mother, Tess Jackson, who listened to me as worked through the story arcs in Autumn Antics and came up with some wonderful suggestions that helped make the book better than it otherwise would have been.

To my fellow Blonde Plotters, Kelly Clayton and Gwyn GB for their support and for all the fun we have with our daily chats.

And finally to you, for reading this book and to the brilliant reviewers, readers and my friends on social media for sharing news about my books, I couldn't do this without you.

AUTHOR LETTER

Dear reader,

Thank you for choosing to read this second book in the Golden Sands Bay series. I hope you've enjoyed visiting Bella's beautiful blue cottage overlooking the sea and accompanying her as she falls in love and finds ways to cope with all that life throws at her.

I love all the seasons but especially enjoyed spending time in the autumn when the leaves change from of green to various golden shades and russet hues and the cooler days and nights begin.

Next in the series is Winter Whimsy and that will be Lexi's story, I hope you enjoy her story.

Until next time,

Georgina x

MORE FROM GEORGINA TROY

We hope you enjoyed reading ***Love Begins at Golden Sands Bay***. If you did, please leave a review.

If you'd like to gift a copy, this book is also available as an ebook, hardback, large print, digital audio download and audiobook CD.

Sign up to Georgina Troy's mailing list for news, competitions and updates on future books.

https://bit.ly/GeorginaTroyNews

Explore more wonderful escapist fiction from Georgina Troy:

ABOUT THE AUTHOR

Georgina Troy writes bestselling uplifting romantic escapes and sets her novels on the island of Jersey, where she was born and has lived for most of her life. She has done a twelve-book deal with Boldwood, including backlist titles, and the first book in her Sunshine Island series was published in May 2022.

Visit Georgina's website: https://deborahcarr.org/my-books/georgina-troy-books/

Follow Georgina on social media here:

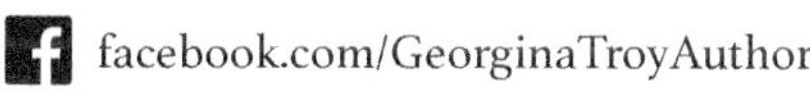
facebook.com/GeorginaTroyAuthor

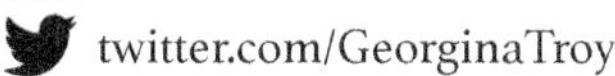
twitter.com/GeorginaTroy

instagram.com/ajerseywriter

bookbub.com/authors/georgina-troy

Printed in Great Britain
by Amazon